Falling For The Wrong Hustla

Tina J

Copyright 2019

Warning:

This book is strictly Urban Fiction and the story is **NOT**

REAL!

Characters will not behave the way you want them to; nor will

they react to situations the way you think they should. Some of

them may be drug addicts, kingpins, savages, thugs, rich, poor,

ho's, sluts, haters, bitter ex-girlfriends or boyfriends, people

from the past and the list can go on and on. That is what Urban

Fiction mostly consists of. If this isn't anything you foresee

yourself interested in, then do yourself a favor and don't read it

because it's only going to piss you off. ☺☺

Also, the book will not end the way you want so please be

advised that the outcome will be based solely on my own

thoughts and ideas. I hope you enjoy this book that y'all made

me write. Thanks so much to my readers, supporters, publisher

and fellow authors and authoress for the support. 😲😲

Author Tina J

More books from me:

The Thug I Chose 1, 2 & 3

A Thin Line Between Me and My Thug 1 & 2

I Got Luv For My Shawty 1 & 2

Kharis and Caleb: A Different Kind of Love 1 & 2

Loving You Is A Battle 1 & 2 & 3

Violet and The Connect 1 & 2 & 3

You Complete Me

Love Will Lead You Back

This Thing Called Love

Are We In This Together 1,2 &3

Shawty Down To Ride For a Boss 1, 2 &3

When A Boss Falls in Love 1, 2 & 3

Let Me Be The One 1 & 2

We Got That Forever Love

Aint No Savage Like The One I Got 1&2

A Queen and A Hustla 1, 2 & 3

Thirsty For A Bad Boy 1&2

Hassan and Serena: An Unforgettable Love 1&2

Caught Up Loving A Beast 1, 2 & 3

A Street King And His Shawty 1 & 2

I Fell For The Wrong Bad Boy 1&2

I Wanna Love You 1 & 2

Addicted to Loving a Boss 1, 2, & 3

I Need That Gangsta Love 1&2

Creepin With The Plug 1 & 2

All Eyes On The Crown 1,2&3

When She's Bad, I'm Badder: Jiao and Dreek, A Crazy

Love Story 1,2&3

Still Luvin A Beast 1&2

Her Man, His Savage 1 & 2

Marco & Rakia: Not Your Ordinary, Hood Kinda Love 1,2

& 3

Feenin For A Real One 1, 2 & 3

A Kingpin's Dynasty 1, 2 & 3

What Kinda Love Is This: Captivating A Boss 1, 2 & 3

Frankie & Lexi: Luvin A Young Beast 1, 2 & 3

A Dope Boys Seduction 1, 2 & 3

5

My Brother's Keeper 1. 2 & 3

C'Yani & Meek: A Dangerous Hood Love 1, 2 & 3

When A Savage Falls for A Good Girl 1, 2 & 3

Eva & Deray 1 & 2

Blame It On His Gangsta Luv 1 & 2

Naima

"Explain why you're mad at me because your restaurant isn't up to par? I mean how am I to blame?" I folded my arms across my chest and shifted my weight to one side.

"Bitch, every time you come here it's something wrong?" The man said.

Each time I came here I think he was more and more arrogant, ignorant and downright disrespectful. I'll never understand why black men never had a problem putting down black women; yet, if I were a white women he'd be too scared I'd close this place down and keep his mouth shut. Maybe I should do that and see if he still calls me out my name.

"Bitch?" I questioned with my face turned up. Also, why do men always reference women as such when things aren't going their way?

"Yup and like I said." He was becoming angrier and just by his stance I backed up a little in case he decides to accidentally hit me. I don't know him, but you never know with people these days.

"The last time you cited me because the got damn light in the freezer was out." He barked.

"How can employees see without it? The freezer is long and deep…"

"I told you then, the light guy was coming that day and asked you to come back. You told me no and gave me a fake ass citation." This man was so mad split flew out his mouth each time he spoke.

"Again, how are your employees able to see if..." He cut me off. I was trying to tell him it wasn't safe even with someone standing there. The person could get locked there and not be able to find their way to the door without a light. He wasn't trying to hear anything I had to say.

"Either someone stands there with them and holds the door or they take a flashlight in with them like usual. Tha fuck you think this is?" I was at work so me laughing in his face for the dumb ass response would be inappropriate.

If you haven't figured it out, I'm a health inspector for restaurants, diners, nursing homes, schools and other places people consume food at. I've encountered people from different walks of life who have been just as disrespectful as this man in front of me. I've met people who have no problem fixing the issues and then I have the ones who throw out threats if I don't pass their place of business.

The things people will do and say to keep their spots open would blow your mind. Now I'm all about making money but if the place isn't up to par then I have to do what I have to; otherwise my job is on the line and I worked too hard to get where I am. I'm not about to lose anything because these individuals can't run their business correctly or their employees can't or don't listen.

"Are you serious right now?" I asked the man who's standing in front of me still upset.

"What? You never had people hold the door for you if a light wasn't working?" He looked me up and down.

"I don't know why I asked when I can tell you're one of those women who know absolutely nothing about living in the hood, not having food to eat and..." I cut him off.

"Sir, my upbringing has nothing to do with this restaurant not being up to code. I'm sure you want me to pass it because we share the same skin color but let's be clear." I picked my things up and headed for the door.

"If you want respect, you need to give it."

"What bitch?"

"Exactly. Since I've been here you called me a *Bitch* twice, told me I should've waited the last time I came for the man to fix the light, as if I'm on your time. You've insulted my job, my upbringing and assumed I'm supposed to be ok with this type of behavior. Sir, as of right now at." I tapped the screen on my phone to see the time. I had things to do and didn't want to be late standing here arguing with him.

"As of right now this restaurant is shut down until further notice. Have a great day!"

"OH HELL NO!" I felt this getting outta hand, put my hand in my purse and took out the mace. He froze.

"It may not be a weapon to kill you, but this type of mace isn't your normal kind. Nah." I shook my head.

"See, I know people too sir and the stuff inside this small can will do a lot more damage than you think." I was lying. It was regular mace, but it still could do damage if I sprayed enough.

"What the fuck eva. Get your stupid ass outta here."

"With pleasure." I hit the alarm on my brand-new Porsche truck, tossed my things inside and looked to see him standing there with two other people.

"Oh, I forgot to mention. If you decide not to listen and open regardless, I'll make sure this spot gets closed forever. See you soon." I closed, locked my door and sped off. This day didn't go as planned.

****

"Bitchhhhhhhh, you keep fucking with these people and someone's going to whoop your ass." My friend Ivy said as she laughed listening to my story.

Every Monday we met up for dinner and Friday after work we'd link up for drinks. Today we stopped at a restaurant I trusted. The guy here is very nice and I've never cited his spot; therefore, I wholeheartedly had no issue eating here. Plus, they had the best chicken Marsala I've ever tasted.

"Girl please. He kept calling me out my name and thought because I'm black he's supposed to pass with flying colors." She shook her head.

"Why did the spot fail?" She asked.

"Two of the soap dispensers in the women's bathroom were empty, someone smeared shit in the men's room and housekeeping didn't clean it enough for my satisfaction." She turned her face up.

"Exactly! You could still see remnants in the stall."

"That's gross." She turned her face up the same as I when I saw it.

"Yup. As far as the kitchen, it was perfect. The place was so clean you could probably eat off the counters." I told her being honest. It was a gorgeous club slash restaurant but with a man like him working there, I'd never think about eating in it.

The floors were like a black marble and the tables were all booths. They had dangling lights above the spots and the seats were comfortable. The bathrooms were just as nice besides the two things needing to be cleaned and the bar was very well kept. There was even a huge dance floor with walls around it to keep customers from running into one another if they weren't dancing. Its hard to explain but very nice. The only problem with the restaurant is the ignorant ass man who runs it.

"So why you fail him for the bathrooms? Bitch, even I know you could've waited for them to fix it."

"You're right and I did it because he was a dick. Had he been nicer and respectful I would've waited and passed it."

"Oh well. He'll learn next time." She said and started eating her salad.

"He will because I told him it's closed until further notice." She almost choked.

"I know Ivy. I'm not supposed to do that, but he pissed me the fuck off." I took a bite of my Marsala.

"You're crazy." I picked my phone up and opened the app that alerted me when someone came to my house.

"Not as crazy as I'm about to be. Look at this shit." I pulled the cameras up in my house and blamed myself for the stupid shit I put myself in.

"Let's go bitch." She requested for the waitress to bring the check and in minutes we both hauled ass to my house in our vehicles.

We pulled up and I stared at my four-bedroom house. I purchased this a few years ago and sadly allowed my man to move in with me. I paid the mortgage and he paid the utilities. He had to be responsible for something being he rested his pathetic head here every night. I wish I knew then, what I knew now.

Mario was Spanish and handsome as ever. He could make some banging ass Spanish food and his sex was great. However, he had three baby mamas and every time I turned around, one in particular Lina, was always calling him for this or that.

Over the last two years, it's been nonstop drama. I'm talking almost fighting Lina, to Mario having another kid on me with her. Devastated and betrayed can't even begin to describe how I felt finding that out. I can't forget the two times he gave me Gonorrhea and said it must've come from one of the public bathrooms.

Through it all, my dumb ass stayed with him for all the wrong reasons. Yes, I loved him, and I didn't want anyone else to have him. I didn't wanna hear another woman claim him as her man, nor did I want him making love to anyone but me. I don't know how many times my mother and friend Ivy cursed me out and told me leave him alone. For some reason I just couldn't.

Now here I am standing outside my house where he let some bitch inside. He knew my routine with Ivy, so I guess he decided to do what he wanted. Today, was the day I had, had enough and he needed to go.

"Go head Ivy. I got this."

"Fuck that. I ain't going nowhere." I laughed.

"Ok just wait in your car then. If I need you, I'll call." It took her a few minutes to agree but when she did, I stormed up to my door and barged in. No one was downstairs, yet the television and every light in the house was on. He must think because he pays the utilities, he can leave all of them on.

I walked up the steps and heard voices. I thought they'd be fucking but imagine my surprise to see him lying in the bed shirtless and the same baby mother he cheated with, was going thru my closet. Neither paid attention to me.

"Babe, she got a lotta nice shit in here. Damn! These shoes are bad." She told him as she tried them on.

"They are right?" I said making both of them jump.

"Naima what you doing here?"

"Last I checked, I lived here."

"When is the last time you checked because to my knowledge this is Mario's house; pretty soon our house. Ain't that right baby?" She sashayed over to him in a pair of my shoes and leaned over to kiss him.

"Let me talk to you Naima." He told Lina to sit down. The minute she did, I pounced on her, grabbed her hair and drug her down the steps. She was kicking and screaming.

"Let her go Naima." Mario had his arm around my neck almost choking me. He has never put his hands on me.

"Bitch, I'm gonna fuck you up." She tried to come towards me but she hit the floor fast when Ivy punched her.

"You got ten seconds to let my girl go." She had her small nine out. Mario pushed me out his grip and smirked.

"Your girl has ten seconds to get out my shit." He started helping the bitch off the ground.

"This my shit so you and her need to bounce before I let Ivy shoot your diseased dick off." I was so mad my body was shaking.

"You got it confused Naima."

"No, you do." I told him and opened the door. He went into my office, grabbed some paper and handed it to me. I glanced over it and sure enough, the deed to my house that I worked hard to get was in his name.

"How the fuck did you do this?" I handed the paper to Ivy.

"Having a big dick works wonders for stupid bitches like you." He said smugly.

"What?" He stood in my face.

"After I fucked you last week, I told you your homeowners' insurance was going up and needed your signature. Guess who signed it?"

"You tricked me?" I questioned because after all the shit he's taken me through how could he do this to me? How could I fail victim to dick and sign over my own house?

"I'll be right back. My lawyer is about to fix this." Ivy said and ran outside to grab her phone from the car.

"Now get the fuck out."

"You bastard." I started punching him in the face and all over his body. He literally knocked me on the ground and drug me out by my feet. I gripped the door and wouldn't let go. I swear it felt like De Ja Vu in that first Tyler Perry movie. The only difference is, he kicked me out my own shit.

BOOM! I heard a gunshot and looked to see Ivy holding her gun. She let another shot off and barely missed his ear.

"Get yo stupid ass off my property and take your dumb friend with you. She lucky I'm not pressing charges."

"FUCK YOU NIGGA!" Ivy shouted and helped me off the ground.

"Nah. Tell your friend not to let good dick fuck with her senses. Dumb bitch." He slammed the door and I sat there looking stupid. How the fuck did this happen?

IVY

"I'm gonna need to know right now what the fuck happened." I said to Naima and took a seat next to her on the sidewalk.

After Mario slammed the door, she remained seated as if something was gonna change. Not only did he trick her into signing over her house, he put his name on her truck and made himself a co-signer on her bank accounts. I don't think she paid the second page any mind but I damn sure did.

I'm a tax lawyer and even though what he did is criminal, I understood everything on the paper. Don't ask me how he persuaded anyone to do this. I mean Mario had the forms notarized too, which meant he wanted to make sure to make it was all legit. The only think I couldn't understand is why my friend is still sitting here? In the last three minutes, the motherfucker shouted if we don't leave, he's contacted the police.

"We have to go." I told her and stood.

"This is my house Naima. Why would he do this to me?" Her eyes were turning red from crying, she had one shoe on and the other one must've fallen off when he drug her out the door.

When I saw him doing that, I couldn't fire off quick enough. Then inside he had his hands around her throat. I swear if my freedom wasn't worth it, I would've taken his life right then and there. I'm not a murderer but I'll be damned if he puts his hands on her.

"I know and we're gonna do everything to get it back." I tried consoling her but how can you comfort someone in a bind like this?

"Let's go." I put both of my hands out and helped her up.

"I should've known this would happen." I didn't disagree because Mario has been doing foul shit to her for a while now. Me and her mom saw straight through his ass and warned her thousands of times, but a woman knows when she's had enough. It's unfortunate it took this long for her to see it.

"All my things are in there. My clothes, shoes, purses and..."

"YOOOOOO!" We heard and turned around. Mario came towards us with a duffle bag.

"Here." He tossed it at her feet.

"What's this?"

"Your laptop and whatever papers you had in the desk. My girl said she don't need it." He had a smug look on his face.

"WHAT?" Both of us shouted.

"Yea the clothes and shoes fit because y'all are the same weight, height and shoe size."

"I want my clothes Mario." He laughed.

"Any and everything in that house belongs to me now. Therefore; the things you purchased even down to that sexy ass lingerie you tried to surprise me with is hers. I can't wait to see her rock it. I saw a pair of heels you brought that will go perfect with it too."

WHAP! Naima smacked the fuck outta him. I pulled my little gun out quick. His hands went up because he knew I wasn't playing and will use it.

23

"Fun fact Mario." Naima chuckled.

"You may have taken my house but if I call the cops right now and tell them I lived here, legally you'd have to go down to the courthouse in the morning and get an eviction letter. Then, the judge would tell you I had thirty days to vacate the property. Sooooo, you and the little bitch would have to wait until then to sport my shit." He ran his hand over his head like he was thinking.

"I didn't think of that but it's all good. You'll just hear me fucking her half the night anyway. Be my guest."

"You're right and I'll find a nigga to do the same. At least I know he won't give me diseases." He jumped and I dared him to hit her.

"How the fuck you mad when you got a whole bitch in there? Let's go Naima."

"That's right. Leave bitch. Don't let me catch you on my property again." Naima tried to turn around, but I held her and kept her looking straight.

"Don't say shit. He wants you to act up." I closed the door when she got in and prayed, she didn't jump out before I pulled off.

"I can't wait for karma to get your ass."

"Don't threaten me with your family members bitch." I stopped and looked at him. This nigga dumb as hell.

"You good?" I asked my girl after closing my door and speeding away. If I didn't, one of us may have jumped out and tried to kill him.

"What am I gonna do?"

"First, you're gonna come home with me, take a nice bath and count the money in your safe." She glanced over at me and smiled.

Naima may have been dumb by accidentally signing away her house for good dick but she's never been a fool when it came to her money. The bank account he put his name on barely had five thousand dollars in it. The one she kept her real money in, had over 400k in it from all the saving she did. Then, every time she got paid, she'd take half out the bank and put it in a safe she kept at my house. No one knew about it but us.

25

"My mother is gonna be pissed. Oh shit! I left my truck." I did a quick U-turn and raced back to the house. Luckily, no one was outside, and she could get it. Her purse, cell and all her other belongings were still there. Both of us drove to my house to figure out her next move.

"Sis, he had the truck put in his name and put him on your bank account."

"He can have that little bit of money, but I'll be damned if he gets my truck." She ran in my office and emailed the car company asking for them to remove his name from the truck. She also let them know they are no longer together and not to put him back on or she'd sue for allowing him to do it in the first place. After she calmed down, I had her take a bath in my spare bedroom and relax. It's been one hell of a day.

****

"You want me to fuck him up?" My man Cat asked me. His real name is Joseph but because he had cat eyes its what everyone called him.

He and I have been together for about four years and we've had our share of issues, but we made it through. He loved Naima like his sister and asked a hundred times if he could beat Mario up.

"You know Mario will call the cops on you. Then who's gonna give me what I need if you're locked up?" He stopped rolling his blunt, placed it on the nightstand and walked over to me by the bathroom.

"Tha fuck I tell you about that shit Ivy?" Cat hated for me to mention another man or even joke about one.

Sadly, my body always reacted to his aggressiveness, so my pussy had already begun to get wet when he walked to me. He snatched my hands, lifted them over my head, used his knees to spread my legs, pulled his dick out his boxers and plunged inside me.

"FUCK CAT." Whenever I made him mad, he'd restrain my hands so I couldn't scratch, dig or push him off.

"Say that shit again." He whispered in my ear as he savagely fucked me against the wall. He wasn't raping me and the rough sex has never been anything less than amazing.

"Say what? Oh shit." I released my nectar on him and watched the grin appear on his face.

27

"I thought so. When you having my baby?" Right then, I knew I messed up.

Cat has wanted me to have his kid since we first got together. I kept telling him to wait and when we had our issues it was easy for me to avoid it. Now that we're in a great space it's really no reason for me not to give him what he wanted. I mean even though I had money, he brought this five-bedroom house for me, my two Mercedes in the driveway and my bank account is always overflowing from him.

The reason I say I messed up is because we never used birth control and honestly, it's been pure luck, I haven't already got pregnant. It could be because regardless of him using a condom here and there or not pulling out when we didn't, I always had my diaphragm in.

Unfortunately, before I could put it in, I had to open my mouth and get smart. I bet he'll let his seeds flow in my womb and dare me to get rid of it in any way. DAMMIT! How could I be so stupid? I guess this is what Mario meant when he said good dick makes you do stupid shit.

"I know you're scared Ivy. I am too but there's no other woman I want to have my kids but you." He crashed his lips on mine and nothing else mattered.

"I love you Ivy." He now had me on my back, legs over his shoulders and staring down at me with the most loving eyes I've ever seen.

"Should I tell him about Wendy or wait until this orgasm passes?"

Wendy is his annoying ass ex who can't seem to let go. Yes, all men have them and unless the woman is in a new relationship, most of the times they bother the one they aren't with anymore. She's the one who did him wrong; yet, I'm the one getting the backlash of it. Like how the fuck is she mad at me and they were broken up a year or two before I even entered his life?

I don't know how she found out who I was or where I worked but the bitch came there one too many times. I had to get the cops involved because she wouldn't stop. I wasn't scared by any means and the two of us have fought a few times but I'm not about to lose everything I worked for because of

Cat or Wendy. I may love him with all my heart, but a bitch will let him go.

As both of us released, I laid there thinking about the shit I went through earlier with Wendy. I rolled over to say something and he was already snoring. I guess I'll wait.

REMI

"Get yo stupid ass up." I barked at the bitch Monee who I've been fucking for the last year.

"You don't need to talk to me like that Remi." She got off her knees and stood in front of me naked.

"I'm saying Monee. You throw up when I cum in your mouth and you throw up when I fuck you too hard. Is my dick hitting your tonsils when I'm fucking you or something? I mean shit, you even threw up the time I got stabbed in the side and saw the blood. Tha fuck is wrong with your insides?"

"Fuck you. I can't help it if my reflexes kick in at the wrong time." She had her arms folded.

"Move." I pushed her to the side and as usual her dramatic ass fell on the bed. I picked my clothes up off the floor and began to get dressed.

"Why you fucking me Remi if you always have something smart to say or you make me get up?" I only been in town a good two hours and here she is with the shits. I just wanted to get my dick wet because I had a lot going on this week and hear she is complaining and nagging like she my girl.

"The pussy good no doubt but yo ass gotta learn to hold your damn food down or something. Who the hell wanna be fucking and hear you gagging and not in a good way?" I sat on the chair in the hotel room to put my sneakers on.

"Do you love me?" I lifted my head and busted out laughing.

"It's not funny Remi." She tossed a pillow in my direction.

"Yes it is and I'ma tell you why before I bounce." I rose up out the seat, grabbed my things and walked the door.

"One... I'm outta town or should I say country more than I'm in it; therefore, we see each other every once in a while." She rolled her eyes.

"Two... how or should I say why would I love a woman who has acid reflex when it comes to dick?" She sucked her teeth.

"And third... how can I love a woman who's fucking other people?"

"You told me to Remi."

"I sure did because the way I rip and run the streets, love is nowhere in sight for me." I walked to the door and felt her presence behind me.

"If you stayed around more maybe you could learn to love me." I opened the door.

"If love doesn't come naturally and I have to learn, then it means love won't come and its not real. I'll be too busy tolerating you to find a chance to look for love with you." I shrugged my shoulders and left her standing there.

My name is Remington Stevens III and I'm a player. I love women, pussy, threesomes with bitches only and my favorite of them all; money. Nothing and no one will ever come before my money. When you allow it to happen things began to go wrong and fall apart. I've seen it happen to a bunch of people and I don't wanna be caught up.

Anyway, I'm 26 years old and an ex dope boy or should I say, retired. As cliché as it may sound, I was born into this life in a way. My mother lived in the projects and my father was in jail for the next sixty years for murdering his best friend and a few others. He's been in there for twenty years already which is basically my entire life. The judge threw the book at him to set an example. Little did he know; my pops will be out sooner than he thinks.

My father wasn't in the streets so it's not like I inherited an empire or the streets. Everything I had, my ass worked day and night to get. I'm talking about late nights, early mornings and sometimes no sleep at all. There was no time for girlfriends or falling in love. The only thing on my mind was money because at the tender age of twelve I've seen more than enough.

"Nigga, you stole from me?" Some street dude asked this kid in the alley who couldn't have been any older than me.

"I'm sorry. My mother is sick and we needed food. I'll put it back."

"How you gonna do that?"

"I'll work later days. Please don't kill me." I heard a gun click and the guy placed it on his head.

"AYE!" I shouted to distract him. Who knew he had some big dude around monitoring the area? The guy snatched me up quick as hell and threw me in front of this dude.

"Who the fuck are you?"

"Remi." I tried to say and poked my small ass chest out.

"Why the fuck you out here this late?" I swallowed hard because I didn't have an answer. Honestly, it was hot in my house from the project heat and I needed some air. I heard yelling in the alley and brought my nosy self here.

"I don't know but why you got a gun to his head? He said his mom was sick and he'll make the money back." He looked at me and tilted his head.

"Oh, you tough lil nigga?"

"Nah but that's some fuck shit if you kill him and he's telling you to give him a chance to get it to you. If you kill him, he's gonna be dead and you won't see it anyway. Why not let him prove himself and if it happens again then do what you have to?" He took a step back and stared at me hard.

"You big Remi's son." I thought about saying no but everyone knew who my pops was. He's a legend in the street

35

and not for drugs. He used to do that Muslim stuff. You know dress in the robes, sell the oils, bean pies and newspapers. People respected him a lot because supposedly he'd always spoke knowledge and tried to help keep the kids off the street.

"Yea."

"Hmph. He know you out here tryna save niggas?"

"How would he know if I'm here and he's in jail?" I had a smart-ass mouth and right now probably wasn't the time to have one.

"Smart ass." The other dude said.

"You gonna let him go?" I didn't have time to stand here listening to his BS. If he wanted to kill this kid, he would've done it already.

"I'm gonna give you a pass boy because lil Remi came to your defense but make no mistake." He yoked the kid up by the shirt.

"You have twenty-four hours to have my money or he won't be able to save you." He hit the kid over the head with the butt of the gun, splitting his eye and kicked him on the way to his car. What type of nigga is he?

36

"That's a bitch move." I told the kid as I helped him up.

"He is a bitch. The only reason he acts this way is because he knows his pops watches everything he do." The kid took his shirt off and used it against his eye to stop the bleeding.

"How much do you owe him?"

"A hundred dollars."

"A HUNDRED DOLLARS!" I shouted. At twelve years old that's a lot for someone of our age to get.

"Don't worry about it. I'll take my consequence." I couldn't let him go out like that.

"What do you have to do in order to make this money?" He gave me a crazy look.

"What? Shit, I don't know." I shrugged my shoulders. He pulled these bags of white stuff out.

"Why you tell him you ain't have it?" I was wondering why he claimed to have spent the money but had the product in his pocket.

"I'm tryna find a way to break it down, split it up and make extra money on the side." He said and looked around to see if anyone was listening or watching.

"Why though?"

"That nigga only pays me fifty dollars. Mind you, I'm out here all night risking my life and freedom. Nah, not for fifty dollars; not no more."

"Damn. That's crazy."

"I know but thanks for looking out. I appreciate it." He started walking off.

"What's yo name?"

"Joseph but my mom and the streets call me Cat." I chuckled.

"Cat? For what?"

"I don't know. My mom said my eyes are slinky like a cat and since they're gray, she said it makes sense. People heard her calling me that all my life and followed suit."

"Oh a'ight but why don't I know you?"

"Because I live in a different town. I'm only here to see my father. Him and my mom aren't together, so I spend the weekends at his place." I nodded.

"REMI! REMI!" I heard my mom shouting.

"I gotta go but my house number is 234. Come visit in the morning and we'll figure out a way to do what you said."

"You ever dealt with drugs?" He asked.

"No but we got this." I gave him a pound and ran off to my house. My mom popped me on the head for leaving the house this late and said she understood but next time, to keep my ass on the porch.

The next day, Cat stopped by at 8 in the morning. My mom went to work so it gave us a lotta time to do what we needed. He took out the bags with the product along with some extras. We calculated how much to skim off each bag and put them in separate ones. It wasn't a lot and you'd only notice if you were paying attention. Fiends wouldn't realize it because they'd be too high.

Long story short, every weekend Cat visited his pops we did the same thing. The two of us started making more and more money over the years, which made our names ring bells in the street. Of course the guy started a war between us.

In the end, we won and took over. I absolutely did not take anyone off his team because even though he no longer breathes, they were still his people. Two of them tried to take his spot and found out just because we were only sixteen, we weren't to be fucked with.

Over the years we did the same as other dope boys who retired from the drug game. We opened up businesses, and I traveled the world more than anything. It's not a country I haven't been to yet. I may not have visited every area in each one but I've been there. Cat used to travel with me until he met lil sis Ivy. She was the total opposite of what he's used to.

Cat loved ratchet, ghetto and hood chicks. He got a kick outta them fighting over him. Not Ivy though. Whatever she did had, had that nigga stuck. She tried to hook me up with her best friend because she said her man cheated on her but I'm good. Again, I don't have time to fall for women and I'm never here anyway.

****

"Tha fuck you mean my spot closed until further notice? Nigga do you know how much money is supposed to come in this weekend?" I shouted in my brothers face. When I'm outta town he's in charge.

"Man, the bitch was bugging." I noticed Tara my club manager put her head down. That told me two things. One... he's telling the truth or two... he did something to make her close it. My instincts were telling me it was the latter.

"Where's her card?" I asked so I could call and have this person return.

"She didn't leave one." I walked towards my desk and fell back in the chair.

One of the local rappers was throwing a party here Saturday which is only a few days away. Dude not only paid a lotta money, but he wanted to shoot his video here. We make great money here but it's never a problem to make more. My brother would know that if he wasn't a got damn leech.

The only reason I hired him is because my mother begged me. Don't get me wrong, I'd go to war for him but he swears this is his. Never mind his ass ain't put a dime into this

41

place, let alone sat his ass outside with me and Cat growing up. He was too busy chasing bitches and crying to me about not having money to buy them holiday gifts. No matter how many times I tried to send him to college or get him jobs away from me, it never worked. I guess he figured since she's my brother it would be an easy ride.

"You better hope this shit works." I picked the phone up and contacted my lawyer. It's only one set of inspectors in this entire state so whoever did it had to be from the facility he named. I told him to get on it because there's no way this woman shut me down over bathroom shit. But then again who knows what he said?

"I'm out." The least Ivan could've done is wait until I got off the phone to hear how it went. I didn't even have the energy to get aggravated.

"Boss it didn't happen the way he said. I mean some of what he says is true." Tara said.

"Elaborate." I hung the phone up and offered her a seat. She looked shocked as she should because I don't allow workers in here, regardless if they're management or not. When she explained everything, I was pissed.

"You're telling me she was going to wait for him to have the bathroom done and he bugged out?" I asked confused with the entire story because Ivan had a different one.

"I don't know if she would've, but she did say because he was rude to her, called her a bitch and gave her a hard time she was shutting it down."

"I don't think that's legal." I told her.

"Its probably not, however the bathroom wasn't cleaned at the time so it may be." I blew my breath in the air.

"Well my lawyers on it. Hopefully, he'll get this shit done quick. If not, I'm opening this weekend anyway." She laughed and left me to sit there in my own thoughts. I got enough shit on my plate, now I gotta deal with this. If it ain't one thing it's another.

Naima

"You know damn well you're not allowed to close a restaurant unless it's absolutely necessary." My boss said as I stared out her window. The shit with Mario was weighing heavily on my mind.

After the fiasco at my house or should I say his, I stayed with my best friend. The next morning, I woke up, checked my email from the Porsche dealership and was happy to see they answered and understood the severity of the issue. Same thing happened at the bank. The manager apologized a hundred times because regardless of the amount being low, Mario isn't my husband, nor were we on a joint account; therefore, he should not have been added without my permission.

Unfortunately, my house remains in his name. As dumb as it sounded, Mario was correct about his dick having me stuck on stupid. I never took the time out to read the paperwork and that's my fault. Now I'm out of a house and it's nothing I can do about it. Legally it's my signature and if I want anything in the house, I have to go to court. I'm not about to do all that. At least he gave me my work stuff.

"I know Margie, but he was a dick and..."

"And his boss got a lawyer involved." I snapped my neck.

"Wait a minute! The asshole wasn't the boss?"

"No and between you and me, his boss was furious."

"I'm lost. If he's not the boss, why was he there?" I asked because most places have a boss present to make sure nothing is wrong and if so, they can fix it right away. I could've allowed him an hour to get the place up to par but again, he was an asshole and didn't need to open shit.

"Evidently, they're brothers and he leaves him in charge while he goes outta town." I was shocked because he must've really loved him if he did that.

"Shut up!" Me and my boss are very cool if you haven't guessed. I would never have candid conversations like this with someone I'm not comfortable with.

"His lawyer is someone I went to college with and he mentioned the brother basically lives off him and barely does anything."

"I should've known." I said.

"When the judge asked me what happened, I couldn't answer because you hadn't turned in the paperwork." I put my head down,

"I told him we didn't have any problem with them reopening the spot and that I will re-do the inspection, which I did yesterday. Girl that place is beautiful."

"I know right. Then you get the asshole and he messes it up." We both laughed.

"Anyway, there's some big party at the club tomorrow and guess who's going?" She showed me a flyer.

"Have fun."

"You're coming." She told me instead of asking

"How the hell am I showing up at a place, I shut down? And they went to court to have it re-opened. Yea, doesn't sound like a good idea to me."

"Girl please. It's gonna be so many people he won't even know you're there. Plus, you need this Naima. Don't let that punk keep you in the house." I thought about what she said and dug in my purse to answer my phone.

"Hey ma."

"Where you at? I need a ride." She all but shouted in the phone.

"Work. Where are you?"

"Jail."

"JAIL?" I shouted and grabbed my things. My boss looked up from her computer.

"I'll tell you when I see you. Just hurry up before they send me to the county." She hung up and Margie grabbed her things.

On the ride over I couldn't come up with any reason on why my mom would be there. She's by far one of the most ratchet moms I know but she hasn't dealt with the law since I was little. I still laugh at some of the things she used to do like curse my teachers out even though I was wrong. She fought a few moms if their daughters bothered me and trust, we've jumped a few bitches together too. My mom is definitely my ride or die.

"I'm here for Nyeemah Carter." I told the officer at the front desk. Yes, we have the same name, just spelled differently. My mother wanted a mini me.

"Her bail is five thousand with no ten percent." She smiled

"FIVE THOUSAND DOLLARS?" I shouted. Yes, I had it but it's not the point.

"Let's just say your mom did a lot of damage and she's lucky the judge gave her a bail." Margie and I looked at each other.

"What did she do and do you take credit cards?" I asked digging in my purse to grab my wallet.

"Yes ma'am and I can't disclose her personal information." I rolled my eyes. I know as well as she does, that she can tell me what happened. I didn't even bother getting aggravated with her and took a seat on the bench after paying.

"Bihhhhhh, why ma in here?" Ivy came rushing through the precinct doors. My mother must've contacted her too.

"I don't know and the lady refuses to tell me."

"You want me to get it outta her? I'll throw my lawyer status at her."

"Bitch, you're a tax lawyer."

"She don't know that." All three of us busted out laughing. We sat there for about an hour before my mother came strolling out.

"Ms. Carter, I suggest you stay away from the residence we arrested you at if you want to stay out of jail." The officer walking her out said.

"FUCK Y'ALL. THE NIGGA LUCKY I DIDN'T BURN IT DOWN." She shouted and we rushed her out still not knowing what she did. We did know throwing out threats could get her locked back up.

"Gimme a cigarette Margie."

"Ms. Carter, I'd appreciate if you stop using me for my..."

"Shut up Margie. I don't feel like hearing you whine. Usually it doesn't bother me but after the day I had, it's better to keep quiet." All of us stared at my mom. She's always talking slick, but she's never came at them.

"You ok? Why were you in jail?" My mom lit the cigarette, took a long pull and leaned against the car door.

"So, after you told me what Mario did..." I cut her off.

"Ma, please don't tell me you went there." I hoped she'd say no.

"You got damn right I went there." I was in shock.

"Anyway, this motherfucker let the bitch answer the door and like the ratchet woman I am, I smacked the fuck out the bitch." All of us covered our mouths.

"What? She lucky I didn't make the kid fall out her hand." She took another pull.

"Mario comes to the door barely dressed talking shit so I tased him and laughed as he hit the floor; hard as hell I may add."

"NO!" Margie all but shouted.

"If I shot him, I wouldn't get a bail." She shrugged her shoulders.

"Long story short, when he fell, I jumped on him and started beating his ass. You know I can't beat him awake and moving." I was at a loss for words.

"The bitch started screaming which pissed me off, so I stopped hitting Mario, ran upstairs to get all your jewelry and some of your shoes and clothes. I basically grabbed anything that would fit in the two duffle bags." Ivy and Margie were cracking up.

"I go put them in my car, run back in the house and this bitch on the phone with 911."

"Where was Mario?" I asked.

"On the ground in pain. I punched her dumb ass one more time and set the kitchen on fire. By the time I was ready to leave the cops were there."

"Ma, how did you set the kitchen on fire?" She smirked when I asked.

"You see, there were paper towels and then there was a stove. You put them together and whew! You can do some damage."

"That's what I'm talking about. Nyeemah you should've taken us with you. We could've beat both of their asses." Ivy shouted.

"Don't you worry. I got plans for him." I just shook my head and opened the car door. It's no need to tell my mother to stop because she's gonna do what she wants. It does feel good to know they all had my back.

"Where's your car?" I turned to look at my mother as Margie drove.

"Shirley was the getaway driver. When the cops came, she pulled off like I instructed before we got there." I sat correctly in my seat with my head against it smiling. That's exactly what he gets for doing me dirty and I don't feel bad.

****

"It's packed in here." Margie shouted as we stepped through the doors of Club Turquoise. It's a nice club and like I said before I'd come more often if it weren't for the asshole brother. It wasn't intimate; yet, comfortable.

"Hell yea. Thank goodness I paid for a VIP table." I looked at Ivy.

"What? Cat don't know I'm here."

"Are you serious?" Margie and I both caught an attitude. Whenever she went out and he didn't know, they'd either end up arguing and not speaking or he'd fuck her so good she'd be outta work for two days. Her words, not mine.

"He doesn't tell me every time he steps out." I thought about what she said as the manager directed us to our seats.

Her and Cat aren't the perfect couple and have dealt with their share of jealous women, ex-girlfriends, hateful family members and so forth. Yet, the two of them refused to let the other one go. I actually love their relationship because through all the nonsense, not one time did he put his hands on her. I say that because in this day and age, men speak with their fist more than ever.

"Enjoy ladies." The lady said and left us at the table. It was a decent size and close to the small stage. You could see the entire place and the music wasn't bad.

"This is nice." Margie lifted the bottle of peach Cîroc sitting in the bucket of ice. Ivy told us she had to order bottle service in order to get a table.

"It is." I said.

"Then why you fail it?" Ivy and Margie asked before laughing.

"Fuck y'all. Let's get this party started." I lifted a cup off the table and poured my drink.

"Coming to the stage is the owner of this club, Mr. Remi himself." The DJ shouted on the mic.

"Remi?" Ivy said causing me and Margie to look.

"You know him?"

"Ugh, that's Cat best friend. The one I tried to hook you up with." I didn't say anything because she's been tryna get me with him forever, but I was with Mario.

"When's the last time you seen him?" Margie asked her.

"He's never in town that's why I'm shocked. Oh, you're definitely meeting him tonight." I just shook my head because she was dead set on us meeting.

"What the fuck your bitch ass doing in my club?" We all looked and there stood the asshole I had to deal with a few days ago.

"One... this is not your club and two... why the hell are you even over here? Don't you have some fake bossing around to do?"

"Fuck you bitch. You gotta go."

SPLASH! I tossed my drink in his face and all hell broke loose. This nigga grabbed me by my hair and attempted to drag me out the club. I could hear commotion all over. Ivy and Margie were going the fuck off and out of nowhere I heard a loud crash. All this for a night out? I'll stay in from now on.

Remi

When the DJ called me up on stage, I glanced around to make sure security was in place for the performers. Everyone appeared to be having a good time and I could smell the amount of money being made. It's finna take me a few hours to count it all but it'll be worth it for sure.

Just as I went to speak on the microphone, I noticed a small commotion at one of the VIP tables and gestured for security to check it out. Not even ten seconds later, I saw a man gripping some woman's hair and dragging her out the club. Two other chicks were fucking him up from behind and not one motherfucker even thought about assisting, which let me know it's either my brother or Cat.

I told the DJ to turn the music on and I'll be back. I jumped off the stage, made my way through the crowd and outside, only to find Cat hemming my brother up against the wall. If he's doing that, something bad must've happened because those two never beef. I glanced around the parking lot and noticed three women getting in a car.

"Yo! What the fuck?" I shouted on my way towards him.

"I don't give a fuck nigga. Those are women." Cat was barking in his face.

"I'm sorry bro. I didn't know Ivy was with her." Then it dawned on me why Cat had him hemmed up. His girl had to be one of the chicks, but I know damn well my brother didn't have her hair.

"Let's take this in the office." I told Cat and he let him go.

The three of us went in and straight up the steps. A few people spoke and I told one of the security dudes to tell the DJ to introduce the performers until I returned. Why in the hell my brother decided to act up in the club is beyond me. I don't tolerate that shit with outsiders and I'm not about to do it with family.

"You better have a good motherfucking reason for dragging some woman out by her hair." I yelled. Cat slammed the door and poured himself a shot from my mini bar.

"The bitch who closed us down was..."

"Us?" I questioned. Cat shook his head because he already knew what was about to happen.

"Do you pay bills in this bitch? Do you have your name on any paperwork or better yet, when did you put money into *our* club?" I walked up on him.

"I'm saying Remi she...." Just like him to ignore the question.

"Did she skip out on her bill or cause a scene? Wait! Did she pull a weapon out or something?"

"No but..."

"There are no buts. Unless the chick did something physically to you, and even then, you should've never put your hands on her, you had no business touching her. Do you know how much money I'm gonna have to pay her not to sue and keep this between us?" He remained quiet.

"Nah you don't because it doesn't concern you. It's not your money; therefore, you could care less." He took a seat on the couch.

"Listen here big brother." Cat stood in between and he had every right because I was ready to knock his got damn head off.

"You're my brother and I love you to death, but this is the last straw."

"Huh?" Is he really confused?

"Your services here are no longer needed."

"Hold on. You're firing me over some bitch? The same bitch who got your club shut down?" I shook my head. He jumped off the chair tryna be tough.

"You don't get it. She shut it down because of the way you treated her." I pointed in his chest.

"You. Not me, not Cat, or anyone else. You." I poured myself a shot at this point because he had me on fire.

"I had to pay the lawyer a lotta money to get this place reopened no thanks to you." I let the liquor burn going down my chest.

"No, you're firing me over the shit with Nelly. You've been waiting and we both know it." I laughed.

Nelly is this chick I called my girlfriend in the seventh grade. Yes, that long ago. We weren't in love or anything like that but my friends had a girl so I figured, why not? Anyway, my brother is older than me by three years and she thought he was better looking. She'd come by the house and spend more time in his room talking about bullshit than with me.

At the time I wasn't into sex and kissing is the only thing I'd do. Unfortunately, I slipped up and let Nelly suck me off one night and be my first. The sex was just ok because she not only stayed dry, but the yelling turned me off. Who wants to hear all that the entire time? Evidently, Ivan did because one day I came home late from basketball and you could hear her the second you opened the door. I knew it was her due to the noise. I opened my brother's door and shook my head as he fucked my so-called girlfriend.

Instead of getting mad, I ate the dinner my mom left me in the microwave, took a shower, put my earphones on and went to bed. My body was tired from practicing and I didn't feel like hearing them fuck.

I don't know how my mother found out because she worked nights, but she cursed Ivan out and told him not to bring that fast ass girl to her house again. He had the nerve to blame me. I told him I don't give a fuck who told, he was dead ass wrong. From that day on, anytime I scolded him he brings it up.

"You must've really loved her pussy because you stay bringing her up." Cat said and he had the nerve to get mad.

"Fuck y'all. I don't need this stupid job. I'm telling ma." He stormed out. Both of us busted out laughing.

"He's really gonna be the death of me." I felt the second shot burn going down my throat again.

"Something ain't right with him bro." Cat stared down at his phone.

"What you mean?" He stood up.

"Every time you got something good going on, he tries to destroy it."

"Nah, you think so?"

"Remember the bowling alley got burned down after you told him he couldn't work there anymore. And the laundromat power outlets kept getting messed up each time the electrician fixed it until you got him this job. I hate to say it, but Club Turquoise is next." I nodded and pulled on my goatee.

Shit definitely happened to my businesses when he got pissed. When I'd bring it up my mother would say he had no need to, but Cat and I knew different. Because I haven't caught him red handed, I can't accuse but he's definitely a suspect.

"I'll kill him."

"If Naima doesn't beat you to it." He chuckled.

"Naima? Who's she?"

"The chick who tossed the drink in his face, is Ivy's best friend and the one who closed it down."

"Word?"

"Yup. He went over to their table talking shit and called her a bitch." He passed me his phone to show me the message his girl sent. I laughed because she was going off.

I handed it back and wrote myself a note to send the woman an apology note and maybe some flowers. I don't need her coming in again and closing me down for Ivan.

The two of us went back out to join the festivities. I'm gonna speak to my moms about him. He can't work in any more of my establishments especially, when crazy shit happens afterwards.

****

"You better not throw up." I told Monee as I gripped her hair tighter. She was on her knees giving me head this morning before I went to Maryland. I had to make a quick run to check on the nightclub I had down there and pick up money.

I'm out the game but I still have a little thing going on the side for these little young niggas. I'm showing them the ropes and turning it over. I just wanna make sure they're ready because my name is on the line.

"I'm not. I took a Prilosec first." I almost fell over laughing had she not deep throated me.

"Fuckkkkk! Keep going." I stared down and a few minutes later, pulled my dick out her mouth and came on her face. She loved that shit. I don't know why when she hates swallowing.

"Why you pull out? I told you I took a pill." She came out the bathroom wiping her face.

"I don't give a fuck if you took a Prilosec, Tums, Pepto Bismol or whatever else is out there. I ain't got time to hear you throwing up."

"Whatever. Can we fuck?"

"Nah. I'm in a rush but thanks." I zipped my jeans up. She should've known I didn't want to because I still had all my clothes on.

"Really Remi?"

"Hell yea really." She rolled her eyes.

"Don't pretend you're hurt because we both know you kicked dude out so I could come over. Matter of fact, how you ready to fuck and had dick in you last night and possibly this morning? I know your hole is bigger than normal but damn."

"Who said I fucked him?" She caught an attitude; yet didn't address her wide ass pussy.

"The empty condom wrappers in the trash and he left one on your coffee table. No respect."

"He does respect me. More than you."

"Does he take you out?"

"We just started messing around."

"And you already fucking. No respect. Peace." And with that I hopped on the road. I'll deal with everything else when I get back.

CAT

"Damn Ivy, a nigga ain't ever leaving yo ass. Shitttttt."
My girl was literally sucking my soul out. She has always been good in the bedroom but when she knows I'm mad or about to dig in her ass for some stupid shit she did, she would fuck me real good.

"Mmmm hmmm. I know what you like daddy." She stopped sucking, slid her tongue down and licked under my balls. I had to grip the sheet because it felt so good.

"Got damn." I stopped her, put her pussy on my face, spread her ass cheeks and returned the favor. We were now in a 69 position seeing who could make the other moan the loudest.

"Catttttt. I'm about tooooooooo...." She never finished her sentence once my index finger slid in her ass. Cum was shooting out all over my face. Her clit began to thump and the wave she experienced was returning.

"Oh fuck." I moaned out when she started humming on the tip. Shortly after suctioning her cheeks, she removed all the seeds I had in my body.

I was still grinding her pussy on my face and sucking on her clit. Ivy can have multiple orgasms but there's one that always hits her the hardest which is the second one. I felt it coming, stopped, sat up and mounted her on top.

"Ride this motherfucker." I had my hand around her throat and the other was circling her pearl.

"Oh shit baby. Shit. I'm cumming."

"I know. Let go Ivy." I placed my mouth on her neck and when she was about to cum, I thrusted harder from the bottom.

"Yes. Yes. YESSSSSSSSSS!" She screamed and fell on the side of me. I gave her a few seconds to get it together, lifted her leg, placed myself back inside and continued hammering away.

"Ok Cat. I'll tell you the next time." She grabbed the sheets, got on all fours and threw her ass back.

"You better."

"AHHHHHH!" I dug so deep she jumped off my dick.

"What?" She punched me in the chest.

"I told you it hurts when you do that." She hopped out the bed, ran in the bathroom and closed the door.

"FUCK!" I slammed my hand on the bed. Ivy is very petite compared to me and the only time we had an issue in the bedroom is when I did that to her. I promised not to do it again and after walking in on her crying, I felt like shit.

"I'm sorry Ivy. I forgot and..."

"Just go."

"Fuck that. I ain't going nowhere." She stared at me.

"I told you I'm not her and you continue to treat me the same. I'm tired of it. I should've told you I was going out, ok. But I can't do this no more. I'm done." She pushed me out the way.

"I know you're not her Ivy. I said I'm sorry."

"It's always you're sorry. You're sorry she fucked you over. You're sorry you called me her name not once but twice after sex. You're sorry she keeps attacking me when she sees me. You're just a sorry nigga."

"What you say?"

"Nothing. Just go." She got in the bed and balled up in a fetal position. I sat down with my head in my hands tryna find a way to fix this shit. I loved the fuck outta Ivy and I'm not about to lose her.

"Please go Cat. I can't do this anymore." The pain in her voice was killing me. I grabbed my shit, walked over to where she laid and leaned down for a kiss. She stopped me.

"Go to her Cat. It's where you wanna be."

"You know I don't want her."

"I don't know shit." She went back in the bathroom and locked the door. As bad as I didn't wanna leave it's probably for the best.

****

"What's wrong?" My mom asked when she stopped by. We were very close, so she knew when something bothered me.

"I messed up with Ivy again." She slammed her keys on the table.

"What you do now? You're gonna stop stressing my daughter in law out." I smiled. Her and Ivy were tight too. I explained the situation and she smacked me on the head.

"Are you tryna lose her? Do you want another man to get her?"

"HELL NO!" I barked. Thinking of Ivy with another nigga enraged me.

"Then I suggest you get your shit together. Get my daughter in law the biggest engagement ring out there."

"Ma, I think she's really done this time."

"Stop letting Wendy win. She may not know but she's the reason you're going through this shit."

"I know." I laid my head back on the couch and stared at the ceiling.

Wendy is my ex who did me extremely dirty. I wouldn't consider her marriage material, but she had been around for a minute. Three years to be exact and the entire relationship was really based on sex and betrayal. Sex because it's the only time we weren't arguing, and she loved being in pain during it. I'm not talking about the pain every now and then during sex. I'm talking about doing hurtful things while we doing it.

For instance, she and I would argue, make up and during sex she'd want me to fuck her until she would bleed after. As I'm doing that, she's using nipple pincher things and I mean they were tight. A few times she asked me to use a whip and beat on her. She had me drip hot candle wax down her back and on her pussy. I'm telling you she's one of those into the dominatrix type of sex. She claims it made her cum hard.

I admit when we first started trying it, I was down because I've never had a chick wanna experience pain in that way. After a while I was over it because a nigga didn't always want rough sex.

The betrayal came from me putting all my trust in her and finding out she tried to rob me. I say try because I don't care how long we've been together, trust with me is hard to come by.

Wendy waited for me to go outta town one night, brought her peoples over and searched my entire spot for a safe. I had one in my house, but she didn't know where.

I was crushed because I never cheated on her and watching her on video help them look angered me. When I returned, she had the nerve to say someone robbed the house, I know it's because it was so fucked up, she didn't have enough time or money to fix it.

I kicked her out and told her not to tell anyone we were ever a couple. My mother wanted to kill her and so did my pops. They weren't together but they were always on the same page when it came to me.

"When's the last time you saw Wendy?" I asked my mom because she seems to run into her a lot.

"The other day, why?"

"When Ivy told me to leave, she mentioned Wendy attacking her every time she sees her."

"WHAT?"

"I know. I'll be back." I ran out the house, hopped in my car and sped over to Wendy's. Shockingly, she was outside talking to some guy.

I blew the horn and waited for her to come to me. I had to adjust myself because her jeans were tight as fuck and her camel toe was showing. Crazy sex or not, she had some good pussy. Just not the kind to make me stick around after tryna rob me.

"Hey sexy. You miss me?" She leaned over and her tities almost fell out the bra.

"Get in." She smirked.

"Let me guess. Your girl ain't fucking you right. You miss the way I used to…" I caught her from tryna grab my dick.

"Get yo petty ass in." She took her time sashaying over to the passenger's side and opened the door.

"Why you fucking with my girl?" I wasted no time asking her. She slammed the door and rolled her eyes.

"Fuck that bitch."

"I swear if you were a nigga talking about her, I would've knocked your teeth down your throat."

"Damn. Its like that?"

"Hell motherfucking yea it's like that." I looked at her with disgust. Not from her being ugly but from her being grimy.

How did I even get myself in a situation with someone like her?

"I'm only gonna say this one time and its up to you if you choose to listen." She folded her arms and pouted like a kid.

"What?"

"You got one more time to fuck with her and I promise on my mother, I'm gonna chop your got damn legs off." She gasped and looked to see if I were playing.

"Cat."

"Get the fuck out my car."

"Why you acting as if you never loved me?"

"I did at one time Wendy and you shitted on me. Now I'm in love with my girl and you're not gonna keep coming for her."

"But she ain't what you want Cat."

"Bitch, you don't know what the fuck I want. Get the fuck out my car."

"She ain't all that anyway." She mumbled opening the door. I know all women called chicks ugly when they don't get their way.

"You heard what I said, and I mean what the fuck I say."

"Whatever. You tell the bitch…" I snatched her back by the hair and slammed her face in the window.

"Oh my God. I think you broke my nose." I could see the blood coming through her fingers.

"You broke it because you don't know how to shut the fuck up." I walked on the side of my car, opened the door and threw her on the ground. I didn't care who saw me.

"Nigga, I can't wait to…" I kneeled down in front of her with my gun under her chin.

"Say it bitch. I dare you." She started crying.

"Don't come for my girl and we'll never have a problem. Do I make myself clear?" She nodded her head yes. I stood and put the gun in my waist.

"Oh, and whoever you think you're gonna send for me; make sure their families have their life insurance policies up to date and their black attire ready because I'll be waiting to put they ass in a grave next to those same niggas you got to try and rob me." I noticed a few people standing out there shaking their heads. Wendy can play tough all she wants but she know what it is.

Naima

"This is amazing. I can not wait to try the steak and shrimp." I told the woman inside the new restaurant Margie sent me to inspect.

The place was by the river with humongous windows to stare out of. There was a long deck leading to an area you and your date could ride the paddle boats on, along with some benches and a gazebo on the way. When you look down the river, houses lined the shoreline and they were nothing short of amazing.

Inside there were two bars and a dance floor. Upstairs held one bar and a small area you could dance in but nothing like downstairs. I'm not sure why it's called a restaurant when it has dance areas but who cares.

Each booth was very intimate with lamps to light them and small jukeboxes to play your own music. Overall this has probably been the best restaurant I've ever seen in my life. I took a few pictures on my phone because there's no way anyone is going to believe me when I mention how it looks.

"Boss man takes his work very serious." She said and escorted me to the small office of hers.

"As should everyone. Here you go." I handed her the paper saying the place could open and picked my things up to go.

"Sorry I'm late. I ran into a problem. Did the inspector get here?" Some guy outta breath yelled into the office. I turned and blushed immediately by how sexy he was.

Whoever this man is had a caramel complexion, faded haircut, and the best set of teeth I've ever seen on a man. He wasn't in a suit, but I clearly saw a print in the dark blue slacks and his muscles could be seen through the polo shirt. He had on what appeared to be Gucci shoes and the Rolex wasn't hard to miss either. DAMN! This man was beyond fine.

"Are you ok? Hello." I heard snapping and brought myself out of the gaze his appearance had me in.

"I'm sorry. I zoned out for a minute." The woman I spoke with about the restaurant had a grin on her face.

"I'm Ms. Carter, the inspector. And you are?" I extended my hand and once his touched mine, I damn near came on myself.

"Mr. Stevens, the owner."

"Oh ok. I must say, this place is nothing short of amazing and I can't wait to try it out."

"Thank you. Are you in a rush?"

"No. This is my last stop for the day." It was after four and I couldn't wait to soak in the tub at Ivy's. Ever since she broke up with Cat a few days ago, she's been crying her eyes out. I understood why she did it but we both know he's not letting her leave him.

"Tara bring Ms. Carter a menu." He told the woman who happily obliged.

"Oh no. That's ok. I can wait until it opens."

"Nonsense. You're here so what's the point in waiting?"

"Really. It's ok Mr. Stevens."

"Here you go and I think this seat would be perfect." Tara smirked and placed us in front of the window. She handed me a menu and winked walking away. Was she secretly trying to tell me something?

"Aye. Get Ms. Carter a drink." He barked and sadly, his aggressive tone continued turning me on. Mario had a bad boy demeanor sometimes but being broke and a loser didn't have the same affect this mans did.

"I'm not drinking at work." He stared at me.

"This is your last spot. Technically you're off." I tried to speak and stopped. It's obvious he wasn't listening to anything I said.

"Thank you." I said to the male bartender.

"This is a tropical sunrise."

"Tropical sunrise?" I questioned because I've never heard of it.

"It's the house special and what Mr. Stevens considers to be the best in here." I smiled because the drink was in a huge martini glass and full of different colors.

"You drink these?" I asked him as he took a seat across from me.

"Not in a woman's glass."

"A woman's glass?" I questioned, unsure of what he meant.

"Men drink outta beer glasses, not wine ones that women wrap their hands around tryna sip and be pretty. I snickered and sipped.

"Mmmm. This is good."

"Wait until you taste the food. My chef is the best." He began pecking at his phone angrily.

"Your chef?"

"Yea. He comes to my house in the morning to make my meals and then whatever restaurant I send him to." I almost choked.

"Wait! You have more of these?" I waved my hand. Why haven't I ever met this man before or even heard of him? Then it dawned on me his brother would've been the one I met anyway.

"I have quite a bit here and in other states." He sat his phone on the table and looked at me.

"Ms. Carter, I may not appear to be smart or business savvy on the outside, but my mind and skills are a dangerous

81

thing." I watched him sip his beer and had to cross my legs. The way his lips wrapped around the tip made me think of what he'd be like in between my legs. What is this man doing to me?

"I know you haven't ordered yet, but Mr. Carter wanted you to try our steak tips as an appetizer." The waiter placed them in front of me. He must've sent them a text because he didn't mention a thing in front of me.

"Ummm ok." They looked delicious surrounded by a small amount of mashed potatoes and asparagus.

"Don't worry Ms. Carter. Whether you can close this establishment down or not, I'd never allow my staff to tamper with your food or anyone else's." I snickered a little.

"It's not that. I was more interested in where's the horseradish? I also wanted to add a little more steak sauce." His facial expression changed.

"Horseradish? A woman after my own heart." He pretended to grab his chest.

"You like horseradish?" He smirked.

"I love all my stuff spicy." My face had to be beet red. This man had no filter and even though it wasn't inappropriate, he was definitely flirting.

"Yo! Get some horseradish and steak sauce out here." He shouted and I saw another employee rushing to the kitchen.

"I have to warn you tho. This steak sauce is my chef's secret recipe. Ain't no A1 shit here."

"I'll be the judge of that being different types of steak are my favorite." He leaned back in his chair and stared for a few seconds. Like any woman, it made me uneasy and he knew it.

"Here you go. Let me know what you think." The chef himself brought it out. I poured it on, dug my fork into two pieces of steak and placed it in my mouth.

"Mmmmm." I closed my eyes and savored the flavor. For a brief moment, all I wanted to do is forget my problems and take as much of this home as possible. I opened my eyes and Mr. Stevens, Tara, the waitress and chef were all staring.

"Ummm. Is everything ok? Was I too loud?" They all laughed.

"I've never seen a woman look more sexier eating food than you did." Mr. Stevens said and the other three dispersed quickly.

"I appreciate the compliment and apologize for the reaction." I slid the out of place hair behind my ear. His phone continued to ring back to back as we both sat there waiting on the other to speak.

"This may be a little inappropriate, but do you have a man? I'd hate to lust after a taken woman."

"No I don't and do you have a woman? I'd hate for a taken man to lust after me."

"Not at all." His phone rang again.

"I have to cut this short, but can I call you sometime?"

"Sure." He handed me his phone, I put my number in it and shortly after, he disappeared.

"I hope you can lock him down." I turned and saw Tara standing next to my table.

"What you mean?" I finished off the small plate of steak tips.

"Mr. Stevens isn't your average man." I wiped my mouth with a napkin.

"He's tough, aggressive at times and to this day, I don't think he's ever had a real girlfriend." I almost choked on my drink.

"What?"

"I've worked with him for the last four years, but I've been around a lot longer. And not one time has he brought a woman around."

"You're kidding right?"

"Some women he may have slept with would stop by stalking him, but he'd kick them out."

"Why is that?"

"He hated for a woman to beg or show weakness but then again most men do. Anyway, he hasn't met his match yet but after seeing how you handled his brother at the other restaurant, I think you're her." She smirked.

"I'm the manager at a few of his places." She smiled again.

"Other restaurant? His brother? Wait! Is he Remi? I mean Remington Stevens III?"

"Yes ma'am he is and I hope to see you around more often and not to close places down." She winked and walked away.

I started gathering my things and couldn't help but smile. Not only did I meet Cat's best friend and he's gorgeous, but he asked to call me. With the way I'm feeling right now, I don't even care if we just fuck. I may go home and pleasure myself tonight off him, that's how sexy he is. I said my goodbyes to the staff and headed to my moms. Today was a good day.

****

"Why are you here Mario?" I asked. He came by my job a few times and after Margie cursed him out, she made him leave. Unfortunately, she's out of the office today and he caught me leaving the restroom.

"I need to talk to you." He grabbed my arm and I looked at him.

"About?" I snatched away.

"In the office. I don't need these bitches in my business."

"Bitches? Only bitch here is you." One of the secretaries said.

"Fuck you punk." Another one said.

"Ok ladies. We're professional here and Mario you need to apologize to these women. They did nothing to you."

"Fuck them. Let's go." He pushed me down the hall and into my office. I turned to speak, and his lips met mine. I pushed him off and smacked the crap out of him.

"ARE YOU CRAZY?" Instead of answering, he reached for the doorknob, locked the door, towered over me, before lifting me up and laying me on my desk.

"Get off me." His mouth was sucking on my neck as his hands massaged my chest. With each second, my body was succumbing to the feeling.

"I miss you so much Naima and if things were different, I never would've hurt you." I lifted myself on my elbows to ask what he meant and fell back when he pulled my khakis down and latched on my clit through my panties. Sexually we've never had a problem and I hated that because he knew just what to do to turn me on.

"Mario. Ssssss." I arched my back, placed one hand on his head and grinded on his face. He stopped to slide my panties off and went full force. I had to cover my mouth, so the women outside didn't hear me.

"Oh shit." I squeezed my legs on his face and came hard as hell. I laid there with him resting his head on my stomach.

"I wanna make love to you so bad but I've disrespected you enough." He helped me sit up.

"Nothing I've done hurtfully in the past is because I wanted to." I hopped off my desk and he walked with me in the private bathroom to clean up.

"I just stopped by to say I'm sorry for everything and even though I don't know what's going on, I had to save my kids." I pulled my pants up and looked at him.

"Are they ok?" I loved his kids even though the one baby momma irked the shit outta me, the other two were cordial and had their own things going on.

"For now. Do me a favor Naima." He wrapped his arms around my waist.

"Be careful and always pay attention to your surroundings."

"Huh? What's going on?"

"I wish I could tell you. Please take care of yourself and don't let anyone tell you you're not worth anything because you are. I love you." He hugged me one last time, kissed my lips and was gone with the wind. I know I shouldn't care if he died after the way he treated me, but I can't help but to feel bad.

I packed all my things up, walked out the office and everyone was staring. I smirked, gave them the finger and went about my business. I'm gonna sleep well tonight.

Mario

"Did she fall for it?" My girl bombarded me with mad questions when I walked in the house.

I was supposed to go to Naima's office and make her talk to me. I did that and more. Unfortunately, I'm gonna have to get her here so these people can take her, which was the real purpose of stopping by even though I never got the chance to say it. When I saw her, all I wanted to do is apologize and make love to her. I'm having a hard time with this shit these people want me to do.

Why in the hell did I bother with this Lina bitch? It's been nothing but problems since I stuck my dick in her and she wasn't even a side chick yet.

"Yea."

"Ok so now what? Is she gonna come over?" I walked up the steps and removed my shirt on the way.

"You better not have fucked her Mario. That wasn't part of the plan." I turned and she stopped short.

"First off, I know the plan. Second... I damn sure don't need you following behind me yelling about where I stick my fucking dick." I moved closer.

"You don't want me fucking her or any other bitch; yet, you're standing here in the house she bought, clothes she purchased and fucking the same nigga she tried to keep you from. So tell me again the difference from what you're doing?" She rolled her eyes like I knew she'd do.

Lina is my third baby mother and down for whatever. Her sex is good, and she birthed one of my daughters and my only son. Out of my three baby mothers, she has to be the only one I wish I never fucked with. However; ever since these people contacted me about Naima, she can say the plan is ok but being anywhere around my ex without her is like poison.

It's no secret Naima is competition for her and had I not gotten caught up in some bullshit behind Lina, I'd probably still be with her. She's the woman any man would love to have on his arm.

Naima is thick as hell in all the right places and she can fuck me straight to sleep. She can cook her ass off and worked

91

nonstop to save up and travel before settling down and having kids. It's always been her dream to see the world and here I am about to destroy it all.

I tried various times to back out but then my kids were threatened. As much as I wanted to save and even tell Naima, I couldn't. Motherfuckers were watching my every move and tapped my phone.

In the beginning, I didn't cheat on Naima because honestly, I fell in love with her. I wasn't concerned about her making more money than me. In these days women definitely doing their thing. Plus, I have a job as head custodian in one of the hotels. It may not be much but I damn sure made enough to pay bills and take her out to nice places.

Lina has my oldest daughter and now my five-month-old son. She and I were history just like my previous baby mothers who were both in different relationships. All of us were cordial and showed up for all the kid's events with no problems. They don't bother Naima and vice versus. Lina on the other hand is where the issues started.

Her stupid ass family had beef with Naima's who I knew nothing about. She was mad I didn't want her anymore then began running her mouth to people on the streets about my girl. She caused major drama with us and I had enough. I went to Lina and begged her to stop but she wouldn't.

Long story short, Lina's people came in, sat me down and started threatening me about making it right with her. It wasn't until I declined did the real reason surface. Then they involved my kids and the choice I thought I had was stripped away.

I did everything in my power to make Naima walk away. I cheated nonstop, brought her back a disease twice, by accident. Lina must've been fucking around and gave it to me because she's the only one I cheated with. I stopped giving Naima money and the sex was there but still nonexistent at times. Being the good woman she is, she stayed.

It took a lot in me to trick her into signing the house over. Throwing her out hurt more when I saw the look on her face. She worked hard as hell to get the place and we celebrated the entire weekend. We christened every room and threw a house warming party. However, I had to take it away in order to save my kids. These people have plans to do other shit to her but again, I couldn't open my mouth, or my kids would suffer.

"I'm just saying Mario. We in this together because..." I yoked her up.

"Because nothing. You were being selfish, hateful and bitter. You got me and my kids caught up in your bullshit." I pushed her away from me and went upstairs.

"Mario I'm sorry."

"Sorry don't stop these motherfuckers Lina. Nothing's gonna stop them until they kill Naima." She rolled her eyes.

"You must be a fool if you think they're not gonna come after us next."

"They won't." I waved her off because she had no idea what these people are capable of. Neither of us did. Family doesn't mean shit and you'd think she'd know that because they threatened all four of my kids, and two are by her.

"Let me make you feel better." I stepped in the shower and let her kiss me with Naima's pussy still on my breath. At this point, I don't give a fuck about how disrespectful it is. She put us in this situation and now I have to figure a way to get outta it.

****

"I did what you asked." I told the guy on the phone. I hadn't heard from them since I took the house from Naima.

"We saw you got the house, but she still has something we want."

"What is it and where would it be?" I questioned hoping they'd tell me so I could get it and get them out my life.

"Its at her mother's place. The only problem with that is, you'll only get it if you knock down the bedroom wall."

"WHAT?" I shouted in the phone.

"Mario, you have to do it. The kids are in danger and…" Lina said rubbing my arm. Was the bitch listening to him talk because he wasn't on speaker?

"SHUT THE FUCK UP BITCH! YOU"RE THE REASON WE"RE IN THIS."

"Tsk, Tsk, Tsk. Not the way to treat your future wife." I looked at Lina.

"I know you didn't tell them we're getting married."
She shrugged her shoulders and picked at her nails.

"Look. I don't know how to get in her mom's, but I'll
figure it out. Is that all? I mean, will you leave my family alone
after I get it?" I needed him to say yes. I didn't have people
who could watch over my kids, so I prayed every night he
didn't touch them.

"You have my word and oh! I'd watch the bitch sitting
next to you. She's not to be trusted." I turned my head and
Lina was scrolling through her phone.

"Be my guest to finish her when its all said and done."

"Your wish is our command. Now hurry up and get the
item." I guess he wasn't feeling her either.

"I don't know what I'm looking for."

"You'll know when you knock the wall down." He said
and I stopped him before he hung up.

"You guys have more manpower than I do. Why can't
you do it?" He laughed in the phone.

"You have no idea who Naima's family are, do you?"

"She has some people in her family I don't care for."

Her cousins and a few uncles were in the streets when we first

met. I don't know if they still are and really didn't care.

"Exactly. Just know she's being watched as well, which

us why we haven't been able to touch her or her mother

ourselves." I heard the beep signaling the call was

disconnected and looked at Lina. What the hell is really going

on?

Remi

"How's he doing?" My mom questioned me about my pops. The two of them were still together when he got charged with murder, but he refuses to allow her to visit. She has hundreds and probably thousands of letters from him over the years because those two stayed in contact that way and on the phone.

He says no woman should come to a jail and neither should kids. However, my grandmother didn't listen and brought me up there once or twice a month before she passed away. I was seventeen when Diabetes took her and sadly, I couldn't see my pops again until the age of eighteen. He was very strict about my mother not bringing me or my brother.

At first, I assumed he had other women coming to see him. Come to find out, he didn't want her there because of how he saw correction officers, other inmates and even some lawyers treating female loved ones who visited. He loved my mother to death and if anyone bothered or disrespected her in any way, he'd probably get the death penalty.

Muslim or not my pops didn't play when it came to family. He believes in taken care of each other and not letting outsiders destroy or tear down your family, which is why I could never understand Ivan and how he acts towards me. You'd think I'd beat his ass a lot when we were young but nope. He's hateful for no reason.

"He's good. Reading a lot and doing the normal working out. You sure I can't get you to send him a picture?" She used to send him photos and stopped about seven years ago.

"I would love nothing more for him to see me but if I can't see him, he doesn't need to see me." She slammed the pot on the stove. It's always a touchy subject speaking on him.

"My bad ma." I walked over to the sink.

"He misses you too and I don't blame him for not wanting you up there. Those men are like vultures and if we want him to come home it's best you stay away. We all know how he is over you." I rubbed her back.

"You think he's still like that?" I gave her the side eye.

"Let's just say, some things never change." She turned to hug me and stopped when a noise came from the living room. We both walked in and wouldn't you know; this nigga had the nerve to be tryna sneak a chick out.

"Ivan what are you doing and who is this?" The woman refused to turn around.

"Ma, you know I have company." Yup, he still stayed with my mom, yet wanted to be a boss.

"Ok but it's seven in the morning and if she's leaving it means she stayed the night. You know damn well ain't nobody having sleepovers or fucking in this house except me." He had the nerve to get mad.

"A'ight ma damn. Can I get her out the house first?" He snapped.

"Nigga, tha fuck you talking to like that?" I was about to knock his ass out, but my mom stopped me. I don't play that disrespectful shit; especially, when it comes to my mother.

"Remi?" I heard and sucked my teeth when the bitch Nelly turned around. I knew her face because the only thing different is the plastic surgery on her ass, stomach and probably chest.

"Still fucking her huh?" I laughed because about eight years ago, I ran into her and she begged to suck and fuck me. I never told him because he's under the assumption I want her.

"Bye Nelly." Ivan basically pushed her out the door. My mother's face showed nothing but displeasure and we both knew it.

"Why are you still sleeping with the same fast ass girl your brother used to date?"

"It was puppy love ma and Remi don't care."

"It's about respect Ivan. You don't sleep with your brother's girlfriend. I told you that years ago."

"Lucky for him, he doesn't have a woman. And did you ever think maybe she wanted me all along?" I laughed. Even if it were true, once I told him about us it should've been hands off.

"I'm gonna go ma. I'll see you later." I kissed her cheek and headed to the door.

"Why you here this early anyway?" Ivan spat with sarcasm.

"Going to see pops, wanna come?" He waved me off. He hasn't been to see my father in years.

After my mom told him about this very situation with Nelly, my grandmother took us up there and my father beat his ass. I mean punched him in the chest, face and slammed him. He said, only fuck niggas do what he did and as the oldest, he knew better. Ivan swore he'd never visit again, and he stuck to his word. To this day, he won't even get on the phone if my father asks to speak to him. Punk ass motherfucker.

****

I drove to the prison talking to the lawyer about my father's case on Bluetooth. Evidently, someone set my father up and even though he did murder one or two of the four people he was charged with, someone else did the rest.

The murder weapon was never found, and they only went off witnesses. See back then there were no cameras, cell phones or any other technology to corroborate his story.

Therefore; he had to sit in jail for two murders he didn't commit.

Two months ago, some guy was arrested and placed in witness protection. During the time he made a confession with a disguised voice detailing the entire ordeal. The case is going to be heard again by a new judge in a month or two and hopefully after hearing the evidence my father will be a free man.

I parked in the lot and hung the phone up with the lawyer. I had a half hour before the visit started so I went through the cameras at my businesses on my iPad and stopped when I noticed a familiar face purchasing a soda. *Why in the hell is she at a laundromat when she's a damn inspector?*

I know how much money she makes, where she lives and how long she's been working. I did a little research but no too much. The most I really checked for in a woman is warrants, robbery, name and face changes; shit like that. You can never be too careful. I wanted a person to give me their own background.

I picked my phone up, dialed the number and waited for her to answer. I could see her staring at the number tryna decide if she should pick up the phone.

"Hello." Her voice gave me chills for some reason.

"How are you?"

"Who is this?" I decided to fuck with her.

"You go around giving your number out to that many people?"

"Excuse me!" I snickered watching her get upset and put her hands on her hips.

"How many people do you give your number to or how many in the last few weeks?" She thought about it for about five seconds and smirked.

"If this is who I think it is, no I don't give out my information to random people. Although, I did entertain this gentleman a few weeks ago, gave him my number, and never received a call." I had to smile when she did.

"My apologies ma'am. I've been extremely busy with the restaurants and my club."

"Busy man huh?" She leaned against the wall.

"You can say that?"

"Well, at least it's not because I left a bad impression."

"Not at all. Since I have you on the phone, what's up with seeing you tonight?" I ain't have shit to do and I'm always down to try new pussy.

"Ummm sure. Where do you want to meet?"

"Your spot is good."

"Yea that's not gonna happen." Her voice had a little frustration in it.

"I thought you didn't have a man." She ran her hand through her hair.

"I don't. It's complicated and I'm not comfortable discussing my situation with a stranger." I nodded even though she couldn't see me. I respected her privacy and didn't pry.

"Listen ma. I'm gonna be straight up."

"Ok."

"I'm just tryna fuck. A relationship isn't what I'm looking for so if you not down let me know."

"Hold on." She took the phone away from her ear and I could see her fingers scrolling. Two minutes went by and she picked it back up.

"I reserved a room at the Marriott. See you at seven."

"Word?" I asked and shocked she didn't hesitate.

"Word."

"Talk to you later." She disconnected the call and I could still see her on the cameras. I laughed and turned the iPad off to go in the prison. Two more months and hopefully that's it.

****

"Your mom still being difficult about sending pictures?" My dad asked with a grin on his face.

"She said yo ass ain't getting shit if she can't see you." He shook his head.

"She misses you pops."

"I know and I miss her too. A few more months son and I'll be outta this place."

"You need anything?" I asked because sometimes he'd ask for books to read.

"Nah. How's your brother doing?" I blew my breath out, sat closer to the table and explained what's been going down.

"He's jealous son."

"What? Nah. Why would he be? He don't want for shit, still lives home with ma and has a decent bank account."

"Courtesy of you."

"What you mean?" He smiled.

"Everything he has is because his brother gave it to him. That motherfucker ain't ever have to work for shit. I mean he worked in a few of your spots but wasn't shit his." I rubbed my goatee and listened to him.

"How can I put anything in his name when he fucks up when I put him in charge?"

"Exactly. If he wanted to make sure you succeeded, he would do whatever necessary to do it. Instead he's taking the jobs and sabotaging them."

"I didn't even look at it that way."

"I blame your mother for asking you to get him a job. He ain't never put in work or got his hands dirty. He doesn't

107

know what it's like to see your visions come to life. He's too busy chasing pussy and paying for things with free money; your money." I knew exactly what he was getting at.

"Ma would kill me if I emptied his account or took his car."

"Remi you're my son and I love you and Ivan the same but he ain't wrapped too tight." I started laughing.

"Anyway. When y'all bringing home grandkids?" I stopped.

"You can ask your other son because this one here ain't bringing home shit." He stared at me.

"FIVE MORE MINUTES!" The CO shouted.

"In all these years you still haven't settled down or gave out your seeds?" He always asked why I didn't have a woman.

"Hell no. These bitches out here ain't worth feeling my dick raw."

"She's coming." He stood and stretched.

"What's that supposed to mean?"

"It means there's a woman out there somewhere waiting to make you fall in love." He laughed.

"I'm good." We gave each other a hug.

"When you do meet her make sure your fucked up ass brother don't try to sneak and fuck her." Both of us busted out laughing. We said our goodbyes and headed in different areas of the jail. On to the next thing.

Naima

"I'll have another one." I handed the waitress my glass. It was nine o clock and I'm at the hotel bar alone.

When Remi called me earlier it was nice hearing his voice. He had a calm aura surrounding him on and off the phone. It's like we were meant to meet.

I'm not gonna lie, I had tons of thoughts about sleeping with him after meeting the first time. That's why I had no problem reserving a room when he laid it on the line about only wanting to fuck. It may sound nasty to some, but a bitch needed some dick and since Mario is a no go, I thought why not?

The jokes on me because we were supposed to hook up at seven. Here it is two hours later and not only am I alone but on my third glass of red wine. The two patron shots I had in between were slowly beginning to creep up on me. I ended up downing the red wine, paying the bartender and leaving. If I'm gonna start feeling tipsy, it's best I'm in my room.

I took my time walking there because it was quite a few men in the bar, and I didn't need anyone following me. After Mario told me to pay attention to my surroundings it made me paranoid.

I unlocked the door, dropped the keys, my purse and phone on the table, kicked my shoes off and went straight to the jacuzzi. This suite was nice as hell and even though I got stood up I'm gonna enjoy it

KNOCK! KNOCK! I heard banging on the hotel door in the middle of my relaxing. I figured the person was at the wrong place because it stopped. Closing my eyes, I turned the music back on my iPhone and went back to relaxing.

"You weren't gonna answer for me?" I jumped up fast as hell.

"DAMN!" Remi said after roaming my body. I snatched the towel off the side and stepped out.

"How did you get in here? And I thought you weren't coming." I went in the room and felt my body being swung around.

"Don't ask questions and I apologize for being late."
He tilted my head back and leaned in to kiss me. Once our mouths connected, lust and anticipation took over.

I pushed him on the bed, slowly unbuttoned his shirt, pushed it off his shoulders and lifted the wife beater off as well. His body was magnificent if I must say so myself. I don't care how corny it sounds and if I'm only gonna sleep with this man tonight, I'm making sure it's a night he'll remember for a very long time.

I heard the distinct sound of the belt I took off hitting the floor, laid him back on the bed and climbed on top. Our mouths met again and this time I grinded my lower half on his. I placed kisses down his neck, all over his chest and found the spot I've been looking for. He lifted himself so I could get his jeans down and the sight made me gasp due to the thickness and length.

"You good ma?" He attempted to get up until I slowly slid him in between my lips.

"Got damn Naima." I sucked him off so good, his dick started twitching in no time. I knew men loved for women to taste their cum so I waited for him to get closer to his peak. When I noticed his body stiffen, I used both hands like a shaker, sucked with all my might and brought him to ecstasy. For extra affect, I kept some in my mouth, spit it back on his dick and swallowed the rest.

At this moment, my pussy was soaking wet, clit was throbbing and I myself was ready to cum. As he laid there tryna catch his breath, I rubbed the tip up and down my slit. I could feel my orgasm brewing and he knew it too because he jumped up, threw me on the bed and in one thrust entered me with so much force I almost lost my breath.

I grabbed the sheets with both hands as pleasure filled my entire body. He moved in closer to kiss me and slammed his hand on the bed.

"I gotta stop ma." He looked at me. We were both still grinding our bodies.

"Why?" I spread my legs apart to allow him deeper access.

"The condoms are in my pocket."

"Ok we'll get them but right now I need this."

113

"Fuck Naima." He stared down at himself going in. The last stroke pulled my orgasm out and had me shaking like a leaf.

"That's sexy as shit." When my body calmed down, I felt another one coming.

"HARDER REMI. FUCK ME HARDER!" I yelled.

He flipped me over and literally fucked the dog shit outta me. He cupped my breast from the bottom and squeezed as he slid in and out. Every stroke he gave intensified the feeling and hit the most pleasurable spots inside. I tried keeping up the pace but with each thrust, I felt overwhelmed with the amount of satisfaction he was giving me.

He buried himself deeper in my tunnel like he wanted to hit the bottom. My body began to jolt, and my senses were telling me it's time. The only thing on my mind right now is releasing this massive amount of pressure. He yanked my hair and pulled my back to his chest. The moans escaping our lips only proved we were both receiving extensive gratification.

"I need to stop but this pussy good as hell. Shit." He yelled and I felt his hand around my throat. Why did it turn me on even more? I dug my nails in his legs and held on because this is about to be one hell of a ride.

"Yessssss. Oh my fucking gawdd. You feel so good." I shouted and came everywhere. He let me go, pulled out and I felt his warm cum decorating my back.

"Fuck! I needed that." He laid next to me and I can't tell you what happened next because my ass was knocked out.

****

"I'm coming nigga." Remi barked in the phone at the caller. It turns out, our one-night stand turned into weeks of nonstop fucking. It's like we were addicted to each other.

"You gotta go?" I walked to the shower in my new townhouse. It took a lot of begging from the bank to get the person to take cash and sell right away. They wanted to move out in a month and so forth but I had to get my own place. My mom's is cool and so is Ivy but after having your own space you don't want to live with others.

"Yea. I got some shit to do. You good?" He stood behind me in the shower.

"I'm good. This ain't nothing new Remi. We fuck, you leave, end of story." He swung my body around.

"How much longer we fucking before you think about letting another nigga slide in here?" I smirked.

"Are you jealous?" He snickered.

"I'll never be jealous over my stuff." He grabbed my pussy.

"Your stuff?"

"Yup. Let me ask you something." He said but never mentioned what he wanted to say. We both washed up and stepped out.

"What did you wanna ask me?" I sparked the conversation back up.

"Oh. My grand opening is in a few weeks. I want you to be my date." I gave him the side eye.

"Fuck it. I'll take someone else." He slid his leg in his jeans.

"I wish you would." He looked up smirking.

"I gave you a look because people are gonna question us showing up."

"And?" He zipped his jeans.

"And what are we? Fuck buddies, a couple, friends with benefits. What? I would like to know how to answer the questions."

"I don't know."

"You don't know?" He was confusing the hell outta me.

"I've never had a girlfriend, well sort of and I'm used to fucking and leaving. Somehow, you get me to stay here, cook for me, sex me good and don't bother me for shit. I mean you do all the girlfriend things, I guess that's who you are?"

"Oh wow. How can I ever thank you for making me your number one?" I went to get some clothes out the closet. He grabbed my wrist.

"A long time ago my brother slept with the only chick I ever claimed." I covered my mouth.

"It didn't hurt because I wasn't really into her but it did make me not trust women."

"That's crazy."

"In any case, you'll be the second one. All I ask is, if you wanna be with someone else; tell me." I let my arms drape around his neck.

"Remi, I'm not her and your ignorant ass brother could never even sniff my pussy, let alone get inside it. If I'm with you, I'm with you."

"A'ight then. You my girl." He shrugged and picked his things up to go.

"When's our first date?" He stopped.

"A date? Ma, we skipped the part where the dates happen first."

"We're a couple now as you say, and I wanna date." I pouted.

"Fine. Set it up and I'll meet you there."

"Remi you have to pick me up." He blew his breath in the air.

"Ok. Ok. Set it up and we'll go together. As a couple. You happy now?"

"Very. Now gimme a kiss before you go." He walked over to me.

"If your pussy wasn't as good as it is, I'd make you come to me."

"Compliment accepted. Have a good day." We engaged in an erotic type of kiss. Fortunately for me, it resulted in him saying fuck the phone call and let me please my girl.

I hope I'm doing the right thing by accepting his girlfriend invitation. I was definitely over Mario but if he's saying to watch my back, is it fair to bring Remi into my drama?

Remi

"Here you go." The waitress sat us down and handed us menus.

"Why didn't we just go to one of my spots?" I asked Naima who had me doing this date shit.

"Because everyone knows you're the boss and would probably be scared to serve you." I looked at her.

"What? When we first met at the new restaurant, your staff came running when you called and I could see how nervous they were. At least here no one will be nervous." I smiled and stared down at the menu. After a few minutes the waitress returned to take our order.

"Since we on this date shit, I better be getting some pussy." She almost choked on her drink.

"I'm serious. You see these prices."

"I don't give it up on the first night."

"You should." I sipped the beer and made sure she was watching. She loved my lips as she says.

"Why is that?" She sipped on her drink still watching me.

"Trying out the dick on the first night will let you know if it's worth it. I mean what if the dick little and he can't fuck? You wasted all that time waiting." She was cracking up.

"Then I'd be mad the pussy trash and probably curse you the fuck out." I tried to keep a straight face, but I couldn't when she was laughing.

Once she got herself together and wiped her eyes from almost crying, she leaned in to kiss me. I hated her kisses could get me aroused instantly; especially when we in a public place. Not that it matters to me because I'd fuck her anywhere. I see her worrying about people seeing us tho.

"What happened with you and your ex?" I asked and she rolled her eyes.

"That bad." She explained in detail what happened, and I had to take a deeper look at the woman in front of me. She's smart and makes her own money but allowed a man to walk all over her just so he wouldn't be with another. It sounds crazy but many women do the exact same thing.

121

"If I continue giving you this good dick, you buying me a house?" She threw her napkin at me.

"I hope you learned a lesson." I started eating my food.

"Yea. Never let dick blind you." I could hear the hurt in her voice. She really loved him and he shitted on her. His lost, is my gain.

"What happened with your brother?" I stiffened up a little.

"We don't have to discuss it if you don't want to."

"It's not that. I just hate dwelling on the shit he did and has done in the past to me. It's like nothing I did for him was good enough. My pops says he's jealous." She reached her hand across the table and touched mine.

"From the little interaction we had at the restaurant, he wants to be the boss and if Margie didn't tell me he wasn't, I never would've known."

"He's not smart enough to be a boss." She put her hands up.

"I'm not gonna argue with that." I chuckled.

"Babe, even if it is jealousy, you have to stop giving him everything he wants; otherwise, he'll never do anything on his own." I stared at her with my fists under my chin. She came over to me and slid in the booth.

"I know he's your brother and you don't want to see him suffer but you have to cut him off." She had me look at her.

"You're the younger brother. He's supposed to be looking out for you. So far, he's slept with a girl you claimed, tried to ruin multiple businesses in your name, probably doing God knows what on the side and babe, he doesn't respect your hustle. At some point you have to realize he's using you and when it doesn't benefit him, he tries to destroy it."

"Is the food ok Mr. Stevens?" The owner who I knew asked. Naima snapped her neck at me.

"What? You never asked if I knew anyone who worked here." I shrugged my shoulders.

"How are you Ms. Carter? I didn't know you were accompanying Mr. Stevens. Had I known you two were here I would've given you the VIP room." She blushed when he smiled at her.

"Don't be tryna steal my woman." I joked.

"I'm too old for a woman her age. She'd run circles around me and spend all my money." He winked at her.

"Let me know if you two need anything. Oh, and it's on the house." He walked away.

"Let me find out you got old men tryna sneak a peek."

"Too bad I'm a taken woman. I may have given him a chance." Now it was my turn to laugh.

"I bet you'd take all his money too."

"Who knows?" She stood and pulled me up with her.

"We all have crazy and fucked up family members. It's how we deal with them that determines the outcome." She stood on her tippy toes to kiss me.

I placed two hundred dollars on the table even though he said it was free. I never want anyone saying they did anything for me.

I went to her house and after we handled our sexual needs, I laid there as she slept thinking about what she said.

Everyone keeps telling me to cut Ivan loose; maybe it's time I did. It would lift a weight off my shoulders for sure.

****

"When do I get to meet her?" My mom asked. I stopped by her house to take her by the new restaurant. I wanted her to see it before the grand opening.

"At the grand opening."

"Why so long?"

"It's still new and I wanna make sure she's the one. I feel like she is but only time will tell."

"And you think you'll know then?"

"I hope so." I opened the door to my new place called Paradise and she gasped. It was the best spot I had in my opinion.

"This is beautiful." She continued walking around.

"Why is there a couch and bathroom in your office?" I smirked.

"You know I work late nights and what if I come her from the gym and need to shower?"

"Mmm hmmm. Well if this woman is all you say I'm sure she's going to ask the same question." She said laughing.

"Whatever. It was here before she came around. And as you say, she may question it but I'm sure it's gonna come in handy for us."

"Boy hush." My mom is down to earth and had no problem cracking jokes with me. I had her sit so we could talk.

"What you think about me no longer funding Ivan? Before you go off, I won't take his car or kick him out your house. I'll even leave the money he has in his account. But going forward I won't give him money, jobs or anything else." I poured her a small glass of red wine and placed it on the bar.

"Honestly, I'm shocked you've done it this long." I gave her the side eye.

"I asked you to give him a job Remi, not to supply him with money and gifts." I thought about what she said and she's right. I just assumed it's what I was supposed to do since I had it.

"You've done great for yourself son. I may not agree to how you've done it, but your father wasn't here, and you stepped up. I love you dearly for it but don't think I want you enabling Ivan." I was about to speak and she stopped me.

"I never said anything because I thought you wanted to do it. Remi." She sat her glass down.

"It's your money and if you're done allowing him to freeload and reap the benefits from your hard work, then do what you need. I would never get upset with you."

"Thanks. I put money in his account last week but that's it."

"Good for you. Besides you need to save up for my new daughter in law." I busted out laughing.

"What? If you're telling me about her, she means something to you." She had a grin on her face. She couldn't wait for me to settle down.

"She does."

"I'm happy for you Remi. Now let's get some grand babies out."

"You sound like pops." She waved me off.

"You two are just the same." I sipped on my beer and thought of Naima. Out of the many women I've been around none of them made me feel the way she does. I done messed around and found a real one.

Me and my mom stayed there finishing our drink and I dropped her off at home before going to my place. I had to grin when I noticed the car in my driveway. I parked, stepped out and went to the door.

"Who said I wanted to see you?" I leaned in Naima's window and kissed her.

"You didn't but I wanted to see you so deal with it." I opened her door and helped her out.

"Why you leave your house like this?" I referred to the long silky robe she had on. I saw the coat in the back but still.

"My man loves surprises."

"You better be naked underneath."

"Maybe. You're gonna have to see when we get inside." I followed behind her like a lost dog. This woman had me stuck and it's nothing I could do about it.

Ivan

"I didn't know your brother would be there." Nelly said
when I stopped by her house. I was tryna get her out my
mom's crib before she woke up that day like I did all the time.

Remi purchased her a humongous one and we stayed
on opposite sides. She never knew I had company and it
would've stayed that way had my brother not stopped by early.
Its really my fault in a way because whenever he went to visit
my father, he'd come over and see if my mom wanted to give
him pictures. She felt some type of way he wouldn't allow her
to see him; therefore, she wouldn't give him any.

Anyway, Nelly and I hooked up after she was
supposedly my brother's girlfriend. I didn't fuck her on
purpose. Shit, she told me they were only friends and being I
wasn't home a lot, how was I to know she was lying? Granted,
she'd be here when I came in the house and stayed over late
but when I was home, she'd be in my room.

The night we slept together, she stopped by the house
claiming to wait for Remi to get home from practice. I let her

in and hopped in the shower. She came in naked and begged to suck my dick. As a teenager, I'm not turning the shit down. Her skills weren't up to my satisfaction, so I had her get up and fucked her instead. The bitch screamed as if I were killing her. However; she was dry which is probably why. I had some k-y jelly, put it on her pussy and it was ten times better. I sent her home with a sore pussy and promised to stay in touch.

When my mom came home, she woke me up out my sleep and cursed me the fuck out. Talking about you don't sleep with your brother's girl. I tried to explain she said they weren't a couple, but my mother wasn't tryna hear it. I blamed Remi for telling and continued fucking Nelly to piss him off. Little did I know, he could care less and even opened the door for her whenever she stopped by.

Over the years Remi became powerful with his best friend Cat due to the drugs they sold. Then, they killed the guy who was running shit and got an even bigger name. The money he was making had a nigga in his feelings because I was broke. My mother tried to get me a job but after seeing the amount of money Remi brought in, I decided no job would pay me the same and sat my ass home. He gave me money whenever I asked and didn't question me on why.

Once Remi became legit and opened businesses, I asked for a job and he let me run each spot when he went away, which was all the time. He loved traveling the world and took me and my mom a few times. The only thing I didn't care for was the way people treated him because he had money. Its like he was royalty even when he was away, and I wanted that same feeling.

You can say I'm a little jealous but to be honest, we wouldn't have what we do had it not been for him stepping up. I should've done it being the oldest but fuck it. I probably would've fucked up anyway.

"That is my moms' crib." I closed the door and sat on her couch.

"Yea, but I never see him." She sat on my lap.

The two of us been fucking off and on for years. She had two abortions by me and I'm the one paying for this apartment. Well Remi is because its his money I'm using to do it.

"Let me find out you want him."

"I have the better brother. The richer one." So what she thinks I got more money than I actually do. My brother makes sure I have a full bank account at all times. He don't wanna hear my moms mouth.

"Let me see what that mouth do because I'm tired of hearing you talk."

"Whatever." She sassed and got on her knees. She took my dick out and started sucking me off. For some reason the inspector bitch came to mind. She may have gotten on my bad side but she's bad as hell. I imagined her being the one sucking me off and became more aroused.

"Right there Nelly. Shit." I was so into it, I pumped harder wishing it was the inspector's mouth I was about to cum in. A few minutes later, I let go and tried to calm my breathing down.

"You came hard Ivan." She stood in front of me naked and again, the inspector was the only one on my mind. Needless to say, I fucked her the whole time imagining the other bitch face. Looks like I'm gonna have to find the bitch and make amends just to feel inside her. I bet her pussy good too.

****

"Have you met your brother's girlfriend yet?" My mom asked when I walked down the steps. I didn't even know she was home. Earlier she mentioned going out with my brother and I didn't expect her home until later. I was actually on my way out to do some investigating among other things.

"His girlfriend? Remi ain't claiming nobody." She smiled.

"He did and from the pictures she's very pretty."

"Who is she?" I pried.

"He said she did the inspection for his new restaurant." I almost dropped the glass.

"I gotta go." I snatched my keys off the hook and drove to my brother's house. I was livid that he decided to make the bitch his woman. Not only did she shut him down but got me fired and threw a drink in my face. Where is the loyalty?

I parked in front of his house and there was another car besides his. I could only assume its hers and parked behind it. I

133

used the key he gave me a long time ago and opened the door. No one was in the living room but I heard voices in the kitchen. Remi too had a huge house and you had to walk in different direction to get to certain parts.

I stepped in the kitchen and noticed the back door opened. I peeked out and she was grinding her lower half on his lap. Her head went back when his hands went up the robe she wore and I can't even front, when she let out a soft moan, I got turned on. I watched for a few more minutes as they kissed and felt all over each other. Just as he went to remove the robe, the music on my phone made both of them jump.

"Oh my God." She rushed to tighten it and Remi sat her on the side of him. I knew he was about to come in and go off. I put my phone up and before I could open my mouth, he punched me dead in the face; dazing the shit outta me.

"Your dick hard from watching my girl?"

"Bro, it wasn't like that?" He must really be into her if he flipping. He didn't even act like this over Nelly.

"Are you fucking crazy coming in my shit and not announcing yourself?" He was fuming and the veins in his forehead were popping out.

"Remi, its ok. He didn't see anything." She tried to get him to calm down.

"FUCK THAT NAIMA! His fucking dick is hard from staring at you." She became embarrassed and ran out the room.

"Why the fuck you here nigga?" He pushed me against the wall.

"I came by to see about the new restaurant." He gave me a *yea right* look.

"Get the fuck out."

"What?" He pushed me towards the door.

"Get the fuck out my house."

"Remi you letting a bitch get in between us?"

"Don't call her another bitch." I saw his fist balling up.

"Then why is she coming between us?" I tried to diffuse the situation but it ain't working.

"Nigga don't pretend its her. If you announced yourself that's one thing but you stood at the door and watched."

"That's not what happened?"

"So you came here with your dick hard?" I couldn't answer because he was right. I shouldn't have watched.

"I love you because you're my brother but if you ever, in your motherfucking life come in my house again and watch my girl, brother or not, I'll kill you."

"The pussy must be real good."

BAM! BAM! The punches were unexpected and landing every time he hit me.

"Remi stop it. Remi please." I could hear the concern in her voice. He finally stopped after fucking me up. I was no match for him and he knew it.

"Ma is gonna love this. Remi beats up his brother for a bitch." I struggled getting up and walked to the door.

"Bitch?" She snapped her neck.

"I saved your ass from a much worse ass whooping and you call me out my name again. Next time, I'll let him kill you. Bitch ass nigga."

SLAM! The door shut in my face.

I walked to my car doubled over in pain. Remi fucked me up bad and had she not stopped him, he probably would've done much worse. Oh, I'm definitely gonna get him back.

I sat in my car and made the decision to head over to the hospital. I called my mother on the way just to start some shit.

"Remi did this to you?" Its like my mother didn't believe it.

"Yea. I went by to introduce myself to his girl and he flipped."

"It doesn't sound like him to just flip. What did you do and why did you go this late?" I sucked my teeth. It was only nine o clock.

"You always take his side. I'm your son too ma, why can't you believe me sometimes? Let me guess, its because he has your husbands name?"

WHAP!

"My husband is your father and his name has nothing to do with anything. Remi loves you and I find it hard to believe he beat you like a man off the street over you stopping by."

"Well he did." She stood there quiet for about a minute.

"The question I have for you is, are you that jealous of your brother you'd make things up to get your point across." I didn't say anything.

"Oh Ivan. Your brother would do anything for you."

"I DON'T WANNA HEAR ABOUT YOUR PRECIOUS REMI." She shook her head.

"I hope whatever jealousy and hatred you have for him, you get over it because I don't like seeing my sons at war."

"Its my fault, right? It always is." She kissed my forehead and told me she'd see me at home.

I called this other bitch I fuck with here to see if she'll be down with whatever plan I come up with to get my brother back.

"Remi did this to you?" She questioned when she arrived.

"Yea. Are you still down or what?"

"Maybe we should leave it alone. If he did this to you, I don't wanna know what he'll do to me."

"Remi doesn't hit women, which is why this plan is easy. So you down or what?" She hesitated but gave in after I promised her money. Bitches do anything for some green. Remi better watch his back because I'm coming for him. Brother or not, he will fall.

Remi

"I'm ok babe." Naima was still tryna calm me down.

"This the same shit he did when we were young." She gave me a confused stare.

"I told you he fucked my girlfriend and after finding out he was watching you, he may have done the exact same thing back then. What the fuck is wrong with him?"

"Remi look at me." She sat on my lap facing me.

"He's not gonna stop me from being with you and I can tell you a million times, I will never sleep with him. Its you and me Remi." I ran my hands over her ass in the sweats she threw on and felt myself becoming aroused.

"I'm not worried about you sleeping with him. I'm more worried about the fact he has some personal vendetta against you."

"What do you mean?"

"He's never come to my house unannounced and regardless of the fact I never have chicks here, he always let me know he was here. He may not have known it was you at first or maybe he did. Whatever the case, it burns me up to know he watched you and got turned on. You're my woman and no man needs to get any sorta feeling off you."

"It is weird babe and I'm a little uncomfortable being here now. I mean what if he walks in again?" I chuckled.

"Trust me. His ass won't return, and the locks will be changed in the morning." I stood up with her still in my arms and went to lock the bedroom door. All the locks were on and so is the alarm, but I wanted her to be comfortable.

"Oh you think we having sex?" She placed soft kisses om my neck.

"Hell yea we are. You got a problem with that?"

"Not if its with you." I smiled.

"It won't be no one else." She laughed until I entered her sacred place. I went in and out slow watching every facial expression.

"Remi, I don't want anyone else touching me. You make my body feel so good." She moaned in my ear.

"Ain't nobody touching you again." I laid her on the bed and we both took each other to ecstasy. Yea, I'm feeling the shit outta her.

****

"Hold the fuck up! You telling me this nigga watched you and Naima?" Cat asked as we sat at the bar. Naima and Ivy were at their regular Friday night spot, so we decided to have a few drinks ourselves.

"The worst part is the nigga was so hard his dick poked straight through his jeans. You gotta be about to bust if your dick busting through some got damn jeans." Cat had his face turned up in disgust.

"Then, he called Naima a bitch. Yo, if she didn't slam the door in his face, I probably would've done him a lot worse."

"That's some crazy shit. What your moms say?"

"She stopped by the next day to tell me he had a fractured jaw, a few bruised ribs, two black eyes and his nose was swollen. Not only that, the nigga told her he didn't know why I beat his ass. I explained what happened and she couldn't believe it."

"You know he gotta play the innocent role."

"Cat, I'm telling you I wanted to kill his ass. Who the fuck watches someone getting ready to fuck?"

"A fucking pervert."

"Exactly! Even though Naima doesn't say too much about it, I can tell it fucks with her when we at the house because she always asks if the doors are locked."

"Now what?"

"Now what, what?"

"You know he's gonna try and get you back." I waved him off.

Ivan is a punk and even if he did try and get me back by burning down my businesses, I can rebuild. He's done a lotta foul shit to me in the past, but this is the worst. I don't know if its because I'm feeling the shit outta Naima or what.

"Hey." I answered my cell that was ringing on the bar as me and Cat talked.

"What you doing sexy?" Naima sexy ass asked in the phone.

"Nothing. What about you?"

"Well, I'm at the door of this bar watching this sexy ass man sip his beer. You know how much I love those lips." I turned around shaking my head. I disconnected the call and licked my lips staring at the fitted jeans and shirt she wore. I pulled her in between my legs and stuck my hands in her pockets.

"You smell good." I stuck my face in her neck. Cat was doing his own thing with Ivy.

"I wear it for you."

"Is that right?"

"Yup." She turned around and put her ass against my dick.

"Who is that?" She pointed in the other direction where Monee stood. I knew she was there and paid her ass no mind.

"Some bitch I used to fuck."

"Ok but why she pointing over here? Remi I'm not tryna fight tonight."

144

"Sit here. I'll be right back." I walked over to Monee and had her come to a corner.

"Why you pointing at my girl?" I had my arms folded across my chest.

"Your girl? When the fuck did that happen?"

"None of your business."

"I don't care about her. When you coming over?" She still tried.

"Read my lips. I'm not. We're done." I went to walk away and she reached for my arm. I saw Naima coming over and pushed her hand off.

"Let's go." I had a grip on my girl because she was ready to fight.

"Fuck her Remi. You know where home is." Monee was pushing it.

"Calm down Naima. She's tryna get a rise outta you." I grabbed her purse and phone and walked out the door to leave.

"Keep that same energy at the house." She sucked her teeth.

"Get in." She did like I asked and waved bye to Cat and Ivy who came out behind us.

"Naima don't let her get to you."

"I tried not to until she offered you an invitation to come over." She was mad as hell.

"You saw me tell her its over and I'm with you. Bitches love to think they got a chance because they see you arguing."

"Yea well as long as your mine, no bitch better have a chance." She folded her arms and kept an attitude the entire ride. I didn't care. All it did is turn me on and make me wanna fuck her harder, which is exactly what I'm gonna do.

Ivy

"Bitchhhhhhh. I'm happy Remi beat his ass." I told Naima when she mentioned Ivan watching her and Remi about to have sex. She told me they were about to get naked had his phone not rang. I'd feel some kinda way if my man had a brother who did some crazy shit like that to me.

I'm actually happy the two of them finally hooked up and she deserved a good man. Its been months since her and Mario broke up and she seemed to be over it. I guess after all the stuff he put her through, she should be.

"I am too but why would Ivan do his brother like that?"

"Bitch he obviously wants you too." She looked at me.

"I threw a drink in his face, shut the club down and watched his brother beat his ass. I doubt he wants me and even if he did, ain't shit happening between us." She was very confident in her response.

"I know that's right. Anyway, how's it going between you and Remi? He's a tough one to crack but you got him wide open from what Cat says."

"Yea well, he's definitely a rough one and standoffish at times."

"All men are in the beginning."

"I know but what if he's claiming me and still weighing his options? Ain't no way in hell he wasn't sleeping with anyone before me he didn't have feelings for."

"Who cares? You're the one he's claiming and taking to his Grand Opening. Bitches are gonna hate on you so bad." I told her and laughed at the same time because its true.

We continued walking through Pier 1 imports. She wanted to pick up some things for her condo. I felt bad because she worked damn hard for her house and the stupid nigga took it. It's partly her fault too for not paying attention but what can you do now?

"How long did it take for Cat to go down on you?" I stopped and turned.

"He hasn't gone down on you yet?" I whispered.

"No. He'll kiss all over me, around it, in between my thighs and anywhere else but once he gets there, he stops." I gave her a weird look.

"The only thing I can think of is he doesn't know how."

"Yea right. As fine as he is." She said picking up some beautiful dishware.

"I'm serious. He's never really had a girlfriend and the one he thought he had, slept with his brother; therefore, he had no one to do it on." She stopped pushing the cart.

"You may be right."

"Or he's waiting to see how the two of you play out and then he'll do it." I told her.

"I'm not saying the sex isn't good because it's fucking amazing; however, I do miss getting pleasured that way."

"Tell him." She snapped her neck.

"Not at all." We both started laughing when some chick walked up to us. I gave her the once over before Naima said she was cool. I don't try and involve myself in drama; especially when I'm a tax lawyer but these women have no respect out here.

"Sooooo, my cousin says he has a girlfriend and she's his date for the Grand Opening. Do you happen to know who she is?" The Tara chick said.

"Ok bitch. He mentioning you in these streets." I joked and Tara laughed.

"Cousin? I thought you only worked for him." Naima seemed surprised.

"I've worked with him for the last few years and I don't mention us being related unless it's necessary. Since you're gonna be around it's only right."

"I guess. Is he really telling people he has a girlfriend?" Naima pried.

"Not really." Both of our mouths dropped.

"Relax. He told his mom, who told my mom, who told me, and I told everyone else." The three of us busted out laughing.

"I knew he'd hook up with you because of how he looked at you in the restaurant." She stopped and grabbed both of her hands.

"I'm not sure how long you two been hooking up but if he told his mother about you, then he's really feeling you. Don't break his heart."

"Shit. You should be telling him that."

"I already did." She winked and walked off.

"You in the family now." She tried to hide the grin, but I saw it.

"He about to eat the shit out your pussy now." She laughed so hard the cart hit the rack.

The two of us stayed in the store another hour, packed her car with the stuff and went next door to Pandora. I wanted one of their soup and salad meals. There meals may be small but they're pretty good.

After leaving there, I stopped by the store to grab some groceries. Cat's mom wanted to stop by and talk. I'm sure he informed her about the breakup, and I don't care. I'm tired of living in the shadows of his ex.

What's really hurting is I know he doesn't want her, yet he can't seem to get her outta his head. I don't know if it's because of how dirty she did him or the fact she won't stop calling or texting.

Of course, she wants him back. He did everything for her as far as bills, purchased her a car and trusted her to stay in his house. The bitch tried to have him robbed and then got mad he kicked her out. As far as sex, I'm into freaky shit but she went overboard with the things she wanted him to do. I'm not letting no man pour hot burning wax on my pussy.

The reason I got upset when he dug so deep from behind is because I'm a petite woman. 5'4 to be exact and I only weigh 140 pounds. Cat isn't small in the dick department, he's about 240 pounds of muscle and I can handle all of him.

However, when he does that pulling out and forcing himself in the shit hurts so bad, I have to refrain from sex for a few days because of the pain. A few times I bled, and the shit pissed me off. It makes me think he's thinking of her because she likes that hurtful type of sex.

The two times he said her name was after sex. He called me her name when I walked in the bathroom and another time when I was laying on his chest. In my head, all I'm wondering is if he imagined her as the one he had been sexing? It's not like he said it in the middle of fucking but still, we had just finished both times. Each time he apologized and swore she wasn't on his mind.

Unfortunately, when you have something in your head it's hard to let go. I don't know if I'm overreacting or not but I'm good with no longer dealing with it.

****

I pulled up at my house, took the bags in, put the food away and took a shower. I loved cooking when I'm comfortable. I poured my glass of wine, turned on some music and started preparing the pork chops.

"Hey mama." His mother said and hugged me. I loved this woman as if she birthed me herself. My mom is around but she gets on my nerves. She thinks Cat and I should be married with a hundred kids by now. I avoid her as much as possible.

"Wine?" She held up a bag holding two bottles.

"I'll never turn those down." I closed the door and we walked into the kitchen. I grabbed her a glass and poured her some of the wine I'm currently drinking myself.

"Let's tackle the elephant in the room." I let my eyes roll in my head. I know she wants me with her son and I wanna be with him but this drama isn't worth it.

"You can stay mad at Joseph all you want but we both know he's not about to let you leave him." When we're having a serious conversation, she calls him by his government.

"And that's a problem."

"Why so?" She asked and sipped her wine.

"Because it's obvious his ex is a factor and I'm tired of being compared to her. Then, if I wanna be in another relationship I have to worry about Cat killing him. It's not fair." I slammed my glass down, covered my face and busted out crying. She rushed over and rubbed my back.

"Look at me." She lifted my face.

"Cat loves you and unfortunately you're right. He will murder any man you try to entertain."

"Why though? Why won't he let me go?" She smiled.

"Have you let him go?"

"No but..." She stopped me from speaking.

"How can you ask a man to let you go and you haven't?"

"I'm trying but...Arghhhhhhhh. Why do I have to love him so much?" I interlocked my hands behind my neck.

"Let's eat." She and I both made our own plates and enjoyed each other's company for another two hours. By the time we finished, both of us were tipsy. I locked the doors, hit the alarm, walked her to the extra bedroom and went to bed myself.

Cat

Standing over Ivy as she slept made me realize she's the only woman I want. I knew it anyway but when your woman mentions breaking up with you forever, shit gets real. All the things you're used to doing with her, she'll do with someone else. All the sexual fantasies she'll have with another man. And overall her presence will be missed.

I smiled when she turned over, thinking about our first meet and greet. It happened when I stopped by a lawyer's office to make sure Remi and my business taxes were correct. They weren't preparers or anything like that, but they'd be able to let us know if it's gonna be a problem when tax season came around.

Anyway, after having someone look over our stuff, one of the lawyers called and said the paperwork appeared fine. However, all businesses should keep a tax lawyer on retainer just in case. I told him ok and asked for the files of the ones who worked at his firm. There were about fifty of them and I had no issue going through each person's file. I wanted to make sure there were no mistakes and our shit would be good; therefore the person should be the best.

The one sticking out the most was Ivy's. She was top of her graduating class, been there for six years and never lost a case. I invited her to dinner with Remi and I so she could meet us face to face. Now I see her name is Ivy Blackmon, and automatically assumed she's white. I mean how many black women have the name Ivy?

Long story short, Ivy showed up and she was a black woman in a bad ass pant suit. Her hair flowed down her back, the Fendi purse was visible and her shoes matched. She was short and her thighs and ass were perfect. Off the bat, I wanted her. Remi knew too because he started laughing and said she's too high class.

Little did he know, after he introduced himself and left us alone, we hit it off very well. Not only was she down to earth but sexy as hell whenever she spoke about business. I was used to ratchet and ghetto, so it turned me on.

Ivy could drop a pen on the floor, and I'd think she was sexy just by picking it up. I loved this woman and I'm gonna do whatever I can to make sure we stay together.

"Mmmm." I heard Ivy moaning in her sleep. I locked the bedroom door because my mom is still here and stripped out my clothes. I removed the sheet off her body and placed my head in between her legs. It didn't matter she had panties on. They were so thin I could eat her pussy straight through the fabric.

"Ssss." She lightly moaned when my tongue slid up and down her lips. Now that she's half awake, I removed her panties, gripped her thighs and devoured her pussy.

"Oh gawwwd Cat." Her legs shook and her nectar shot out on my face. I continued sucking until she released one after another. When I felt she couldn't take anymore, I stood, grabbed her by the ankles, pulled her to the edge of the bed and slowly entered.

"Got damn I missed this." Her nails were digging in my chest with each stroke. I leaned in to kiss her and noticed the tears falling down her face. They always say a woman cries when she has make up sex.

"I'm sorry for hurting you." Her arms went around my neck.

"I don't wanna be without you Cat. I love you and…"

"And you won't." I lifted one of her legs on my shoulder and made love to my woman for as long as she could take it. When we finished, you damn right I laid my ass right in the bed with her. She put her back to my chest and snuggled under me. I ain't going nowhere.

****

"Yo nigga!" Remi and I turned around. We were on our way into a business meeting. Neither of us knew the dude and continued walking towards the building.

"Cat, right?" He shouted. I turned around.

"Who wants to know?"

"I do nigga. You ain't have to do my girl like that?" Right now, I had no idea who he was referring to. I know damn well it ain't Ivy.

"Your girl?" Remi stood next to me ready to beat his ass. Not only did he interrupt us but he talking big shit.

"Wendy's my girl and she told, or should I say showed me what you did. You gotta answer to me nigga." I looked at Remi and the two of us laughed in his face.

"Oh its funny?" I walked up on him.

"Very. Now do me a favor and move the fuck on before you get yo ass beat." I glanced around the area and being its early, not too many people were out here. I still didn't wanna cause a scene but if he keeps talking, I won't have a choice.

"I guess its only right to give your girl the same treatment." That was it. I hooked off and Remi followed suit. We didn't have to jump him and wouldn't have if his friend didn't come running around the corner tryna get in it.

Once Remi saw him, he knocked him out and assisted me in finishing this punk. Their faces were fucked up and I doubt they'd be able to move for a while.

The only good thing about this spot is, I owned the building we were walking in; therefore, the security tapes won't exist if the cops showed up. I picked my phone up and rushed to call Ivy.

"Hey babe." She was cheerful as hell.

"Hey. You good?"

"After last night and this morning, I'd say I was." She always brought a smile to my face.

"A'ight. I'm going in my meeting. You need anything?"

"No and good luck. Y'all got this." She blew me a kiss and said she loved me.

"I'll pick you up after work." I told her because I don't know what these niggas know about her.

"Babe, I drove. Its ok."

"Nah. I'll see you around six. Leave your car."

"Fine but you better be taking me to dinner too." I laughed and told her I'd see her later.

"She got your ass on a tight leash." Remi joked.

"Whateva. Shit, the way you moving I'd say Naima has your nose wide open." He had a doofy grin on his face and kept walking. Its good to see him dealing with one woman.

161

After the shit his brother did all those years ago, I didn't think he'd ever be in a relationship with a woman.

"Hopefully Ivan don't whisper sweet nothings in her ear?" He stopped short and turned with the evilest look on his face.

"Yup. You feeling her." He waved me off.

"She good peoples Remi, just hurry up and get rid of Monee." He wasn't sleeping with her anymore that I know of, but she's been calling, texting and showing up at places nonstop. Naima isn't gonna deal with that shit again after what her ex put her through.

"Naima ain't going nowhere." I laughed when he pressed the button to the elevator. As the doors closed, we noticed cops pulling up. I sent a text to security and went on with the rest of my day.

Remi

"Let me find out Naima got yo ass in love." Cat joked while we worked out at the gym. He stayed talking shit about me and Naima. Ever since him and Ivy made up, he wants everyone to be in love and stuck like him.

"I don't know if it's love but..."

"Negro please. Yo ass invited her as your date to the grand opening next week. You told your mom she's your girl, who told her sister, who told Tara and now the entire hood knows. Then, you got her that expensive ass tennis bracelet from Tiffany's yesterday."

"It's gonna go nice on her hand."

"What the fuck eva. Nigga you in love." I lifted the weight above my chest while he spotted me.

"Why this nigga ice grilling me?" He asked and I put the weight on the bar and sat up.

"Who?" He pointed to some Spanish looking guy.

"You got a motherfuckin problem?" Cat barked. People started looking at us walk to this dude.

"What's up?" The guy was putting gloves on.

"Why you staring? You know me?" Cat questioned him.

"Nah. I did hear you talking about my girl tho." Cat glanced back at me. He's been with Ivy forever and she ain't crazy enough to dip out.

"Your girl?"

"You said Naima, right? Naima Carter?" I folded my arms because he was speaking to me indirectly. He must've assumed Cat messed with her.

"Explain how she's your woman when I'm fucking her every night?" I don't usually answer questions about who I'm with but I'm definitely feeling Naima and I told her if she wanted someone else, to tell me.

"Are you?" He lifted one of his eyebrows.

"I'm not about to entertain your bullshit. We both know you not fucking her. I suggest you keep it moving."

"That's not what she said when I had her laid out on the desk moaning my name."

"Tha fuck you say?" I felt myself getting pissed each time he spoke.

"She must be sucking you off like she does me. Those jaws are serious." All I saw was red after he said that. I beat his ass so bad, not only did the cops have to be called so did the ambulance. Cat couldn't even pull me off.

We left outta there unbothered about anyone reporting us to the cops. Its always good to be cordial with people because they'll have your back even when you don't ask.

"Still think you're not in love?" Cat closed the door and started laughing.

"Fuck you." He put his hands up.

"I'm just saying. Ain't no nigga who only fucking a chick, blacking like that on someone he don't love."

"Yo. I'll kill her if she fucking that nigga. Matter of fact, I'm stopping by her got damn job." I sped off gripping the steering wheel thinking about the shit dude said. I parked in handicapped and went through the doors with Cat laughing behind me.

"Can I help you?" The receptionist asked with a grin on her face.

"Where's Naima?"

"You mean Ms. Carter?"

"Bitch ain't that what I said?"

"Excuse me!" She rolled her neck.

"I'll find her." I walked past her, through the doors and down the hall. I opened up door after door until I found her.

"Ok. What do you want me to do?" She looked up from the phone she spoke on and raised her index finger to tell me to wait. I snatched the phone out her hand and hung up.

"What's wrong? You ok?" She started checking my body, lifting my shirt and making sure I wasn't bleeding.

"What happened to your hand?"

"Some nigga said he fucking you and this nigga lost it." I turned and Cat was going in the bathroom.

"Was it Mario?" I pushed her against the window but not hard.

"Who that nigga?" She pushed me off as hard as she could.

"Remi, I'm going to say a few things and you can go." She moved away from me.

"Mario is my ex and..."

"Did you fuck him in here?" I turned my face up at the desk.

"Something went down in here before your time, but we didn't have sex." She responded without hesitation.

"Why he saying y'all still fucking?"

"Did you do that to him at the gym?" I shrugged my shoulders.

"His mother called and blamed me."

"Fuck him. Are you still fucking the nigga?" I heard the toilet flush. Cat came out a few minutes later and said he'd be outside the door.

"I'm not sleeping with anyone but you Remi and that's stopping so you can see yourself out." She gestured to the door.

"Ain't shit stopping unless I say so." She came from around the desk.

"You don't get to tell me what I'm going to do. I'm grown and if I say we're not, then we're not." She poked her finger in my chest.

"And furthermore..." I cut her off with a kiss, moved against the window sill, lifted that skirt, slid those panties to the side and inserted myself in her. I promised myself not to fuck her again without a condom after the first time in the hotel and I was doing good until this very moment.

"Got dammit Remi." Her head went back as her nails dug in my shoulders.

"Who you not fucking no more?" She gasped each time I hit her with a stroke.

"I can't hear you."

"Shut up. I can't stand you Remi. Ssssss." She moved in circles until she caught my rhythm and that was it. The two of us were so engrossed in the other we didn't hear the banging until it got loud.

"I'll... be right... out." She moaned and bit down on my shoulder.

"You know it takes me forever to cum so if you tryna see who behind the door, you know what to do." I told her and felt her muscles contracting against my dick.

"Just like that Naima." She placed her hands on my ass and my hands were above her head on the window.

"I'm finna cum for you sexy." She threw her tongue in my mouth and I felt the grip on my neck when she came.

"SHIT!" I pulled out just in time and let loose on her legs. I pulled my basketball shorts up and helped her off.

"You can't enter my job throwing a tantrum over something a guy said." She stared at me with an innocent look.

"Remi, I promise you are the only guy I'm with. I'd think you know that by how much time we've been spending together and when we're not, we're on the phone." She stepped out the bathroom with warm paper towels to clean us both up.

"I told you I'm very protective of my stuff." She tossed the paper towels in the trash.

"Your stuff?" Her hands were on her hips. I pulled her into my chest.

"Everything from the top of your head to those sexy feet is my stuff." A grin crept on her face.

"Stop beating people up please." She walked to the door.

"Not that I care, but I do care what happens to you and I don't wanna visit you in jail. I mean how else will I get that?"

She pointed to my dick. I waved her off and walked over to the door when she opened it.

"What's wrong?" She asked Margie who had a nervous look on her face.

"Besides this punk who wouldn't let me in." Cat told her to shut up. I wish Naima entered my life sooner but with the constant travel there's no way we could've.

"This came over the fax." Naima took it from her hand.

"Oh my God!" She shouted, dropped the paper and ran out the door. I picked it up and read it.

I'm coming for you and your mother. The person typed it up and left some damn smiling emojis on it. Who has time to do all that in a threatening letter?

"OH SHIT!" Cat and I both ran out. I opened the door.

BOOM! BOOM! I watched Naima's body hit the ground. I pulled her away from her car that just exploded.

"Naima." Her eyes we're closed and blood was pouring from her head. I lifted her body, placed her in my car and hauled ass to the hospital.

"Yo! Call Naima's mom and tell her to meet us at the hospital." I heard Cat on the phone with Ivy. I could hear her asking what happened.

"Wait! The letter read, *they're coming for her and her mother*. Send someone to get her because we don't know if whoever did this is watching her house." I said. He told Ivy not to make any stops and to meet us there.

"Who the fuck tryna kill her?" Cat shouted and made the call for someone to get her mom. He had to wait for Ivy to text the address because we didn't know where she lived.

"I have no fucking idea but they just woke me up."

****

"She has a concussion, a little swelling on the brain and some bruised ribs. She has some scrapes we cleaned and patched up." The doctor told us. It was me, Margie, Ivy, Cat, a few of our boys and her mom.

"Can we see her?" I asked.

"Yes but she's probably going to be asleep for a while. Follow me." We walked through the doors and thankfully they had her in a private room. Coming to the ER you never know if you'll be in a room or the hallway.

"Shit." I interlocked my hands over my head and stared.

Naima had a tube in her nose, monitors on her chest, two braces on her legs that the nurse just told us is to stop blood clots. She didn't have any but due to the trauma her body endured they wanted to be sure. There was a white bandage wrapped around her head along with some wires coming out the top. Evidently the doctor wanted to monitor her brain activity for seizures.

Her mom ran to the side of the bed and Ivy rushed to the other. Margie stood next to her mom and all of them had tears coming down their face. Cat shook his head while my mind was going a million miles a minute thinking about who could've done this? Did the nigga I beat up send someone to her job? Did she have beef? I kissed her lips and told the women I'd be back.

"What's up?" Cat asked walking behind me.

"I need to find out who sent her the fax and go from there." I stepped out the hospital and picked up my phone that was ringing off the hook.

"Yo!"

"Son, you ok? Thank God."

"Pops. How'd you know?"

"It's not much I don't know in here. The girl. Is she ok?" I was shocked he questioned me about Naima. I hadn't even told him about her yet but then again, my mom does write.

"She's fucked up pops." I hit the alarm on my car. I heard him blow his breath.

"They're coming for her Remi. You have to keep her safe." I stopped short and Cat jerked forward.

"What you say?"

"You have to come see me. There's things I need to tell you about her." He was whispering.

"Hold up. You know her?"

"Something like that. Until you get here, keep her safe. I'll never forgive myself if anything happened to her."

173

"Pops you gotta give me more."

"I can't over the phone. We'll talk." And with the last statement he hung up.

"What the hell is Naima caught up in?" Cat asked looking as curious as me.

"I don't know but whoever did this ain't finished." I dropped him off and told him I'd be back after changing. I can send people to watch her but it's better if I'm there.

Naima

"I guess you didn't die." I heard someone whispering in my ear as I laid still in my hospital bed. The last thing I remembered is getting a fax and running out the door to save my mother.

"Don't worry. I'm gonna make sure the next time you don't make it." I opened my eyes and there stood a man wearing a black mask. How the hell did he get in here looking like that?

"Who are you?"

"You'll know soon enough." I reached down for the nurse's button and pressed it over and over.

"I unplugged it." The person stared at me for a few seconds and before I could react his hands were rubbing on my breasts. I went to scream, and he placed his dirty hand on my mouth.

"In due time I'm gonna have you."

"Why are you doing this?" He had the nerve to kiss my neck.

"It's time you pay for the sins of others." He stuck his tongue in my ear. I tried to move my face, but he held it in place.

"Please stop." Tears were streaming down my face, thinking I'm about to be raped.

"CODE BLUE!" Someone shouted on the intercom.

"Nowhere is safe from me. I will come back for you." The message on the intercom must've scared him because he disappeared and all I could do is cry.

Remi has been to here for the past two days taking care of me and the one time I send him away to get food, this happens. I had to basically beg him to go. He refused to leave me alone and wouldn't tell me why. I wanted him to get fresh air but I see why he didn't want to.

"You better eat this whole cheesesteak since I had to stand in a long ass line." Remi said coming in the room with a bag and two drinks. He switched the lights on and stopped.

"This is exactly why I didn't wanna leave. Fuck! You ok? Did they hurt you?" He dropped the food and drinks on the table and rushed to me. I explained to him the best I could about what happened.

"I'm gonna ask you this once." I nodded.

"Did he touch you?" I shook my head yes.

"Did you see his face?" I shook my head no and hugged him tight.

"Please take me home." I was hysterical crying by now. My body was shaking, hands trembling, and the tears wouldn't stop. He walked out and returned with the doctor.

"Ms. Carter we would like for you to stay a few more nights..." Remi cut the doctor off.

"Fuck that! My girl was attacked while your fat ass nurses sat there eating and running they mouth. I should knock the shit outta them. They know no one is supposed to enter this room." I grabbed Remi's hand because he was mad and ready to hit the doctor.

"Remi please relax." I squeezed his hand as tight as I could.

"I apologize Ms. Carter. I didn't know anything transpired in here."

"It's ok. Can you please discharge me?" I guess he felt bad because he finally agreed and left to do what I asked.

"Put these sweats on." Remi sat me up slow and helped me get dressed. The nurse assisted me in the shower earlier, so I wasn't in dire need of one.

"Ms. Carter, these are your discharge papers and..."

"Bitch get the fuck outta here before I snap your got damn neck." I covered my mouth and felt fearful for the lady. She backed out quick as hell.

"Dumb bitch dropped the papers." I busted out laughing as he picked them up.

"What?"

"You scared the shit outta her. Did you expect any different?"

"Fuck them." He sat the papers next to me and lifted my face.

"I'm sorry he got in here. It won't happen again." I placed my hand on top of his.

"What's going on Remi? Why is someone after me?"

"To be honest Naima, I don't know. When the car exploded and we got you here, my pops called and said I had to keep you safe because he'd never forgive himself if something happened to you."

"Your father?" I questioned because we haven't met. He talks about him all the time because he's supposed to get out soon, but I've never met or spoken to him.

"Who the fuck are you?" Remi barked at a guy dressed in scrubs who came in.

"Ummm, they called and said someone was being discharged. I wanted to know if she's ready." He was nervous.

"I'm sorry about his reaction. He's just worried about me. I'm ready."

"May I?" The guy asked.

"May you what?" Remi was snapping on everyone.

"Remi stop it." He moved away and stood there staring the guy down.

"I'm going to bring the wheelchair in but one of the nurses needs to come unhook you from the IV and check the bandage on your head. There's some blood leaking." I felt my head.

"It's dried up but I can tell right now if they send you home like this it's a possibility your husband would return." Remi smirked.

"He's just overprotective and worried." I glanced down at his hand and noticed his ring.

"I'm sure you're the same with your wife." He smirked and told me he was.

"Ok Ms. Carter. Let's get you out of here." The doctor said walking in and disconnecting me from the machines. I guess the nurses didn't want to come in.

When he finished, I signed the papers and had Remi get my stuff. On the way out none of the nurses looked in our direction and I'm happy. I didn't need my man bugging out.

****

"You do know we not supposed to fuck when your body still bruised." Remi said as I climbed on top.

It's been a week since I been out the hospital and his Grand Opening was set for yesterday, but he changed it to next week. He said he's not going without me. In four months, we have become so close, its as if we've been together forever.

Each day I'm getting better but the headaches are very painful. A few times I had to take four Advil just to get it to subside. My ribs hurt but not as much, and the stitches came out on their own. My body was slowly healing itself and I couldn't wait until I'm 100% better.

"We don't have to fuck. I can just do you." I kissed his lips and took my time pleasing his entire body. He stopped me before I could go down on him.

"Nah. Its time for me to take care of you." He gently flipped me over and kissed me from head to toe. It was so erotic I felt a little nectar slipping in between my bottom lips.

"Remi, you don't. Oh shittttttt." I moaned out when he pressed his mouth against my clit.

"I should've done it a long time ago. Let me enjoy this pretty pussy." I stared down and he was staring up smiling.

"Ok baby. Ssssss." I arched my back a little when he sucked on my pearl and stuck two fingers in. The feeling began to take over and my body was losing the battle. He gently bit down, and I couldn't stop my juices from shooting out if I wanted to. He didn't stop there. Remi had me get on all fours while he slid in the bed under me.

"Give me all that good shit." He squeezed my ass, pulled me closer to his face and had me screaming. I tried to run because I couldn't cum anymore, but he held me tight. And here I assumed he didn't know how to do it.

"You ok to ride me?" He asked. After kissing and tasting my own juices I guided myself down and rocked slowly.

"Yea ma." He smacked my ass. I went faster and rode him harder.

"Got damn you gonna make me cum." He gripped my thighs, bit down on his lip and when I knew he was about to release I hopped off and finished by sucking out his cum.

"I think I'm in love with you." I wiped my mouth with the back of my hand and moved up closer. His arm was covering his face as he tried to slow his breathing.

"You think?"

"I don't wanna be without you and I wake up smiling when you're next to me. I've never texted a woman as much as I do with you and I damn sure don't allow any bitch to stay the night."

"I'm a bitch?" He removed his arm.

"I'm not saying that. What I'm saying is, I'm not sure what I'm feeling because no other woman had me going through this. I mean the thought of you dying had me going crazy. I don't know. Maybe it's lust or something." I smiled, pulled the covers over us and laid on his chest.

"I'm in love with you too and no it's not a rebound one."

"It better not be." I looked up at him.

"I may have still been with him but my love was gone a long time ago."

"So why he saying he fucked you?" I could tell Mario mentioning it bothered Remi.

"The day he came to my office was weeks before you and I hooked up. Granted, I was horny and failed victim to him giving me head, but we didn't have sex. Now that I think about it, he told me to watch my surroundings because I wasn't safe."

"What?" He sat on his elbows.

"He mentioned the only reason he hurt me was to save his kids." I sat up.

"You think he knows who did this?"

"I don't give a fuck what he does or doesn't know. If you see him, go the other way and call me. Whoever's after you could be following him and that's how they found you at work."

"Remi what if they hurt my mom?" I started tearing up.

"I have people I'm cool with at the police station. They have officers monitoring her house 24/7. She good." He had me look at him.

"I've never been in love but now that I am, I'm gonna make sure you're treated like a queen."

"I don't wanna be a queen. I just wanna be your one and only."

"You've been her since the first time I stuck my dick in this banging ass pussy." We started kissing.

"Your ex was right about one thing." I wiped his lips when we stopped.

"Oh yea. What's that?" Why did I ask?

"He said your jaws are serious." I smacked him on the arm.

"Who taught you how to do it?"

"No one. I tried on the guy I first slept with and then on Mario. Each time I'd try different things on him until I mastered how he liked it. I did the same to you."

"Did what?"

"I mastered how you want me to please you."

"Oh yea." He kissed my forehead.

"Yup. You want me to show you some of the things you really like?" I lifted the cover and dizziness washed over me. I know I'm not pregnant because they had to take a test and it came back negative. Plus, we're pretty good about using condoms except a few times.

"You good?"

"Yea. Just a little dizzy."

"You take those vertigo pills?" He reached on the nightstand and handed them to me. I didn't have vertigo, but the doctor said the trauma may have me feeling like I do at times. This must be what he's talking about.

"You think it's too early to be in love?" He asked and handed me a water bottle.

"There's no time limit and if this is your first, it can happen quickly."

"Yea well. Expect to hear jokes because no one ever thought they'd see the day a woman could get me."

"I'd like to think we have a lot in common besides sex."

"We do but the sex with you is a 100% match." I laughed, put the water bottle on the nightstand and cuddled up next to him. It felt good to be in love again. I hope it's really how he feels because I'd hate for him to confuse it with lust.

Cat

"I'm not wearing no peach color Ivy. Pick something else." We were at the Gucci store in New York tryna find something to wear for the Grand Opening of Remi's new spot. Outta all the businesses he had, this is the first one he decided to have a big opening for. I asked him why this one and he said, because it's the biggest restaurant he owns and it's on the lake. I admit it's definitely the best one and he put more time and effort into it.

"Peach looks nice on me Cat."

"Everything looks nice on you but I'm not wearing it and look like a bad piece of fruit." She started laughing and walked over to me.

"You are a bad piece of fruit." She sat on my lap facing me.

"You love this bad piece of fruit." Her arms were around my neck.

"I'm in love with this bad piece of fruit. I love you so much Cat." I stopped kissing her neck and asked what's wrong.

"Nothing. I'm not sure I tell you enough."

"I love you too Ivy and I'm sorry for each time I inflicted pain on you. I'm gonna try not to ever hurt you again."

"Try?" She chuckled.

"You know I accidentally find a way to piss you off." She threw her head back laughing. I put my face in her neck and pretended I was kissing her.

"Two niggas I don't fuck with are here and I'm sure they're strapped." I kept her hair covering my face. It was the two dudes Remi and I beat up for approaching me with that Wendy shit.

"Cat." Her body tensed up.

"Whatever you do, don't act nervous and try to be calm." I noticed the guys walking in the other direction of the store.

"I want you to walk out ok."

"Cat, I'm not leaving you."

"Right now isn't the time to be my ride or die Ivy." I know she's not scared but I also know she's a lawyer and I refuse to place her in a situation to lose what she worked for.

"Cat." I stood her up, handed her things to her and basically pushed her out the door. If I walked out without Ivy they won't go after her.

I headed towards the door and gestured with my eyes for Ivy to keep walking. She may have been out the store but she didn't move from in front of it. I loved her more than myself and if anything happened to her, I can't even tell you what I'd do.

I guess the niggas didn't recognize me. I'm happy because innocent people would've been hurt.

"You ok?" Ivy questioned when we got in the truck.

"As long as you're good, I'm perfect." I pulled out the mall parking lot and couldn't help but see a truck going the exact route. These niggas must've followed us out.

"Babe, I need you to get in the back and get low." No questions asked, Ivy did it just as the back bumper was hit. I glanced in the mirror and saw the truck getting ready to ram into us again.

"Call Remi." I spoke in the Bluetooth of my truck. You heard the phone ring as the truck hit again.

"SHIT!" Ivy shouted. It made me take my eyes off the road for a minute.

"You good?"

"Yea babe. Just drive." I could tell by her voice she wasn't telling me the truth.

"YO! Ivy make you spend 10 racks out there on a dress?" Remi laughed in the phone.

"We got a problem on the George Washington Bridge."

"Say less." Remi hung up and I continued going in and outta traffic fast and careful. If it was just me, I'd be reckless as fuck and would've run them off the road already. I can't take the chance of hurting Ivy, so I'll have to be extra careful.

POW! POW! POW! POW! These niggas were shooting and all it did was fuel the fire brewing in me. I flew through the tolls going into New Jersey.

"Fuck this." I took my gun out and right before I rolled the window down, four cop cars were flying up the turnpike. They pulled them over and sadly sprayed their truck. Well not sadly but shit, it was them or us. That's what happens when you deal with real niggas. This is what you get. The phone rang in my truck.

"You good?" Remi shouted in the phone.

"Yea."

"Is Ivy ok?" I heard Naima in the background yelling.

"Ivy come back to the front." She didn't say anything. I swerved to the side of the road and jumped out. I swung the back door opened and my mouth dropped.

"Yo! I'm going right here to Beth Israel Hospital in Newark. I'll call you in a few."

"WAIT! What happened to her?" Naima still yelled. I didn't have an answer for her and rushed to get my girl some help.

****

"You pacing isn't gonna make the doctor come out faster." My mom said and asked me to sit down. I've been here for about three hours and her, Remi, Naima and Ivy's mom came about an hour ago. No one knew anything besides what I told them.

When I opened the back door, Ivy was leaning over with blood coming out her mouth. I automatically assumed she was shot and sped like a bat outta hell to the hospital. The nurses rushed out to help me bring her in. They took her in the back and I haven't heard anything from them since. The wait is killing me and if they didn't hurry up, I'm going the fuck back there.

The doctor must've heard my thoughts because he emerged from the back and told us to follow him to a corner.

"Ms. Blackmon suffered appendicitis and there was an abscess filled with puss. It formed outside of her appendix and exploded which caused peritonitis."

"What the fuck are you saying?"

"Ms. Blackmon had to undergo emergency surgery to fix it. You're lucky you got here sooner than later because the infection was very bad and could've been fatal."

"Oh my God!" Her mom cried out.

"She's going to be fine but when she gets home, she'll need to avoid all stressful activities. I'm going to suggest she takes off work for a week or two and if any bleeding or extreme pain returns, she needs to get to the hospital right away."

"Where is she?" I asked tryna get to the back.

"She's in recovery right now. Give us about an hour or so and you can see her." He shook our hands and left us standing there in shock.

"Has she ever discussed having pain in her stomach?" Her mom questioned me.

"No." I sat on the seat with my head in my hands thinking about the rough sex we have and the last time I went hard. Did the shit make it worse? I couldn't help but think maybe I had a part in this happening.

"Ivy is stubborn. If she was having pain, she would've kept it from all of us. She hated for anyone to worry about her." Naima said and rubbed my back.

"Let me talk to you." Remi moved away from the ladies. I went to where he stood and leaned against the wall.

"Who are the guys?"

"The ones we beat up before our meeting a while back." He looked at me.

"Exactly! I can't help but assume it wasn't a coincidence they knew I was there but how?"

"This is how?" He showed me a photo from what appears to be Facebook. It was Wendy taking a picture in front of one of the stores. If you paid attention you saw me and Ivy. She must've saw us and sent it to the dudes.

"How the fuck they get here so quick." He gave me a duh look.

"You said Ivy takes forever to shop. If Wendy caught y'all when you first got here, then they had time." I snickered because Ivy would have my ass in the mall for hours. Don't let her be pissed off because then we'd go food shopping and do other shit just afterwards for her to prove a point.

"How did I miss that?"

"You ain't miss shit. You were in a whole different state shopping with your girl. Why would you expect to see them?"

"Yea but…"

"Bro, don't worry about it. Y'all safe and it's the only thing that matters. You know what you have to do though." I nodded. He told me in so many words Wendy has to go.

"I should've done it a long time ago."

"We can't dwell on the past."

"FUCK!" I shouted.

"Relax bro. I don't need my girl panicking."

"You really in love nigga." He glanced over at Naima who was smiling back at him.

"Yea. She got me." I laughed.

"I'm happy for you bro. You deserve it." I patted him on the back and sat there with everyone else waiting for the doctor to come get us. I'll be a lot calmer when Ivy is in my presence.

Ivy

"Ouch." I cried out. I didn't mean to be loud and I knew Cat would come running.

"What's the matter? You ok?" I was bent over holding my stomach.

"I'm fine babe. I coughed and didn't have the pillow next to me." He helped me in the bed and got in next to me.

"You need anything?" He pulled the covers up and made sure I was comfortable before he was.

"I'm ok." I kissed his lips.

When Cat was driving to get us away from those guys, a pain shit through my body like I've never felt before. At first, I thought a bullet pierced my stomach. It hurt so bad, I thought I was gonna die. I didn't tell Cat when he asked if I were ok because he'd worry and probably stop the truck. I figured once the situation was handled then I'd mention it.

Unfortunately, the pain became unbearable and when he asked me the second time I couldn't answer. Blood was coming out my mouth and I couldn't talk. Cat stopped the truck, opened the door and I could see fear in his eyes. He laid me on the back seat, checked me over and sped all the way to the hospital. He held my hand the entire way and begged me not to leave him. I wanted to say I wouldn't but with the pain running through my stomach its no way I could promise him anything.

Once I woke up, they placed me in a room where I had to stay for two days. Cat never left my side; not even to change his clothes. He said, we'd be leaving and he'll do it then. Nothing or nobody could get him to get fresh air or leave to grab something to eat. He was too scared something would happen and he wouldn't be there.

On the day I was discharged, I asked the doctor if I could still have kids because truth be told, I wanted kids by Cat. Maybe not right now, which is why I snuck and took the plan b bill the day after we had unprotected sex. If he knew, he'd probably kill me. I've been protecting myself ever since.

"Remi said don't worry about the Grand opening tonight, you can make the next one." I stared at him.

"The doctor said to avoid stressful activities. Babe, I know how long it takes you to get ready. The process is stressful." I smacked him on the arm.

"I'm going babe."

"I told him you were gonna say that."

"Whatever." I laid in his arms and fell asleep. I'm going to the opening so let me get my nap in.

****

"You look good as fuck Ivy." Cat stood behind me in the mirror.

"Well my man won't allow me to look a mess on his arm." He kissed my neck.

"Hell motherfuckin no. Ivy my dick hard. Can we fuck real quick?" We hadn't had sex since I left the hospital and both of us were horny. We were nervous and tryna wait as long as we could.

"I think my man deserves some extra nasty sex." I turned my body slow and slid my hands in his pants.

"Oh yea?"

"Yea and I'm gonna give it to you when we get home."
I took my hands out his pants and kissed him.

"I want you Ivy." He sat me on the sink.

"I want you too baby but its late and we're supposed to be there to walk in with them in an hour. I promise, I got you."

"You better." He helped me off the sink and the two of us grabbed our things to leave.

"I love you Ivy."

"I love you too and I can't wait to be your wife." He stopped and stared.

"You finally ready to marry a nigga?" Cat asked me two years ago to get married and I told him not yet. After all we've been through and knowing neither of us will let the other go, we may as well take that step.

"I'm ready." He smiled and threw his tongue down my throat.

CRASH! CRASH! We both looked towards the back door where we heard the glass breaking and smoke started filling the room.

"What the fuck?"

"What's going on?"

"These are smoke bombs. Let's go." He opened the door and someone started shooting. Smoke was everywhere as Cat drug me away from the door. I couldn't move as fast with these damn straps up heels and hurt stomach.

"CATTTTTTTT!" Our hands disconnected and before I could go searching for him, my body was lifted.

"GET OFF ME!"

"Shut the fuck up bitch." I heard and felt a blow to my face knocking me out.

****

"Hurry up." Someone yelled. I opened my eyes and a big man was carrying me. I had no idea where we were, and the place seemed secluded. It was dark and you could barely see in front of you.

"Where am I? Put me down?" I started punching his back. He stopped and put me on the ground but not without slapping the shit outta me first.

"Thanks cuz." I snapped my neck to see who was speaking.

"What do you want? Is it money?" I asked hoping they'd say yes and I could go grab some.

"Shut the fuck up." The person yelled.

"Fuck you." My reaction was to talk shit back knowing damn well I shouldn't have.

"You're the one who's fucked." The person pushed me, and I couldn't grab on anything to catch myself as I fell into what appeared to be a ditch.

SNAP!

"AHHHHHHH." I screamed out. My foot had to be broken from the fall. I was scared to take the shoe off because the strap seemed to be keeping it in place a little.

"Awwwww, did you break something?" I could barely scream due to the pain.

"I NEED A DOCTOR."

"The only doctor you're getting is in hell. Welcome to your grave."

"PLEASE DON'T DO THIS." I mustered up all the strength I could and stood. There was nothing to grab onto and with my foot messed up, there's no way I could climb out.

"What you wanna do now?" The big guy asked.

"The shovel is there and so is dirt. Bury her ass alive."

As the first shovel of dirt hit my head, I knew this was it.

Remi

"Its not fair Remi. I've been fucking with you a lot longer. How you find a new bitch to claim?" Monee whined. She had been texting me nonstop and I avoided her at all costs. Most women take the hint when a nigga don't return their call but not her.

The only reason I'm talking to her now is because she caught me coming in Club Turquoise. Its closed for the grand opening of my new spot but I had to grab some papers from here. The bitch must've been waiting here all day.

"First off... don't call her a bitch and second... I've never told you I'd be your man." I grabbed what I needed and shut my office door.

"Let's go." I had her wait downstairs because she ain't my girl and no one comes in my office anyway except Cat.

"REMIIIIIIII!" She whined following me to the back door.

"Wait!" I opened the side door and turned around.

"What?"

"Let me make you feel good real quick." Something was suspect as fuck with Monee. If I tell her I'm out she doesn't chase after me or maybe she does and I leave in such a hurry, I pay it no mind.

"Back the fuck up." She pushed me against the wall and tried her hardest to get my jeans down. When she didn't succeed, her hands went under my shirt. She kissed my stomach and I pushed her off. It sounds like I let her but trust a nigga moved her the fuck back.

"Hold up! You smell that?"

"I don't smell nothing. I wanna fuck Remi." I moved past her and let my senses lead me to the smell. I walked in the kitchen and there was a small fire on the stove. I grabbed the fire extinguisher and put it out. Who the fuck was here? I couldn't help but think about Cat mentioning Ivan tryna sabotage my spots.

"Who tryna set your shit on fire?" Monee questioned as she fanned her face.

"I don't know. Let's go." She followed behind me without tryna fuck which made me stop.

"Oh you don't wanna fuck no more?" I asked to hear her response.

"Fuck it. You said no." *BINGO!* Something wasn't right. I didn't have the time to bother with the shit and locked up.

I called Tara up and had her come to the club with a fire inspector to check it out. I wanted the security footage sent to my phone and told her we'll link up at the opening. I sat in my car and watched Monee hop on her phone immediately. I just shook my head because it meant she was tryna set me up, but why? I drove to my house with many thoughts on my mind. I'll have to deal with it tomorrow.

****

"Mmmm, don't stop Remi." Naima moaned out as I hit it from the back.

"You like this dick Naima?"

"I love it. Oh shit. Oh shit." Her body shook as the orgasm took over. She fell flat on the bed. I turned her over and reentered my new favorite spot.

"Remi we're gonna be late."

"Its my place. We can be fashionably late." She used her arm to push me off.

"In that case, let me go for a ride." I smiled, laid on the bed and placed my hands behind my head.

"Got damn you feel good as fuck." I told her. We finished fucking the shit outta each other, hopped in the shower and got dressed.

"If I don't say it later, I'm proud of you Remi." She looked up at me with those innocent eyes.

"Thank you."

"I mean it. In the short time we've known one another you worked your ass off, and I admire you for it. One day I'm gonna have my own business and I hope I'm as successful as you." I pulled her close.

"I'm glad you're by my side. Besides my mom and pops, there's no one else I'd want there."

"Awww baby."

"And you'll be successful at anything you do." We started kissing again and she moved away.

"You know a kiss lands us right back in the bed. Let's go."

"Maybe you should stop kissing me." I said following her down the steps.

"I love seeing your dick get hard. Your reaction, gives me one and the consequence is always good." I smacked her on the ass.

"Let's see how good it is when we get home later. You wanted it rough earlier and we were on a time limit but make no mistake Naima. I'm gonna give it to you."

"I can't wait." We left the house and arrived hand in hand on the red carpet I had out. Like all places who have grand openings, I had the newspapers, local news and radio station personalities there.

"Baby I'm gonna use the bathroom. Go mingle with your guest but don't get fucked up." I laughed. Naima disappeared in the crowd. I walked around speaking to everyone and making sure the bartenders kept people's drinks filled.

"Congratulations son." I turned around and my pops was standing there in a suit.

"How the hell did you get here?" We embraced one another and for the first time we didn't have to stop. The CO's usually give us a hard time. Not that we wanna hug long but they don't even give you a second to do it.

"I wanted to surprise you. Cat picked me up earlier and I stayed at his place." I figured that because Cat only stayed in his own place if him and Ivy were arguing.

"Where is he? Him and Ivy were supposed to walk in with us." I glanced around and
didn't see them anywhere.

"I'm not sure but how I look?" He did a turn in his suit.

"Good pops. Did mom see you yet?" I think so. He pointed and my mother stood there with tears in her eyes. I had to walk over and lead her to where my father was because her feet must've been stuck. The two of them hugged and wouldn't let go. I thought about letting them go in my office but its been a long time and my pops will probably wanna fuck all night. Plus, only me and my girl fucking in there anyway.

"Good job bro." Ivan said and patted my back. I had no idea he was coming because I hadn't heard from him after I beat his ass and he wasn't invited.

"Thanks." I went to walk away and he said something to make me turn around.

"How you think Naima would feel knowing you were with Monee earlier?" I snatched him up by his shirt.

"What the fuck you say?"

"You heard me. I stopped by Club Turquoise to apologize to you and Monee had you hemmed up against the wall. She must have some good pussy if you risking your so called new love interest."

"I didn't fuck or touch that bitch."

"Son let him go. Hello Ivan." Its like my brother saw a ghost. His eyes got big as hell.

"You may not have fucked her but she took it as an open invitation to come." He pointed to a woman who had the same shape as Monee, but it couldn't be her. I didn't invite that bitch here.

"Pops." Ivan spoke and walked away.

"What's going on?"

"I think Ivan set me up to try and fuck Monee and get this." I ran my hand over my face.

"There was a small kitchen fire in Club Turquoise. Had I not been there it would've grown. I think he did it."

"Get him the fuck outta here before he does something else." Me and my pops walked around looking for him.

"Hey babe." I heard Naima behind me.

"Hey. Have you seen my brother?" Her face turned up.

"Stay close. He's here and I don't want him bothering you." She nodded and intertwined her hand in mine. I was about to introduce her to my father until one of my workers interrupted.

"Boss, we need some more liquor and Tara isn't here yet." I'm the only other person with the key to the cellar where the liquor is. I didn't trust anyone.

"I'll get it Remi." Naima had her hand out for the keys. I was reluctant to give them to her.

"Its ok."

"Remi this is your big night. Stay here with your guests. I'll be right back." I was struggling with letting her outta my sight.

"Watch her." I told one of the bouncers. He followed behind Naima and the worker. I picked my phone up to call Cat and he didn't answer. Where the fuck is he?

"Have you seen Cat and Ivy?" My mom asked. Her and Ivy's mom were together drinking like always.

"Nah. I just called and he didn't answer. Something don't feel right." I told them and both of their facial expressions changed.

"We're gonna go by the house because its not like them to miss anything this big." His mom said and they both gave me a hug.

"Ok and call me as soon as you get there." When they left, I went to find my brother.

"Damn Remi, this is nice." The nightmare I got rid of earlier stood in my face. She looked good but she's not my cup of tea anymore.

"Move the fuck on."

"Why? You don't want your girl to see us?"

"Bitch get the fuck out." I left her standing there and went in search of Naima. She was taking too long to come back. I noticed her talking to Tara and she didn't look happy. I hope Monee didn't say shit to her.

Naima

"Ok, I think we have enough for you to finish the night without having to return." I told the chick Sandy. She's the employee who asked Remi to get more liquor.

"I hope so. These people hear free drinks and you'd swear they were tryna drink for the rest of their lives." We both laughed.

"Let me lock up and I'll be right behind you." She stood off to the side and I told the bouncer he could go upstairs to check on everything. I didn't want him gone too long and Remi get mad.

"Can I help you? No one is supposed to be down here?" Sandy asked someone coming down the steps. I locked the door and turned to see Remi's ignorant ass brother.

"Ms. Carter and I know one another, and my brother don't care if I come down here." Sandy didn't know what to say.

"We're ok Sandy. Let Mr. Stevens know we should be good for the night." I told her she could go. I wasn't about to portray how nervous he made me.

"What can I do for you Ivan, or Mr. Stevens?" I stood there with my arms folded.

"Let me be the first to say, you are stunning in this dress." He walked around me licking his lips.

"You're nowhere near the first person to say it but thanks." I gave him a fake smile.

"I'm sure."

"Anyway, I wanted to apologize for the way we met. I was wrong and a man should never treat a woman that way. I also apologize for watching you at my brother's house." He licked his lips like the creep he is. *So he was watching me.*

"Its ok. Is that all?" I went to walk past him, and he grabbed my wrist.

"My brother seems to be in love with you, which is weird because he's never felt this way about any woman." My heart fluttered when he mentioned Remi loving me. I was nervous giving him my heart but to hear him verify it only made me happier.

"I'm glad he feels the same as I." I took a step forward and he stopped me again.

"You know, I think its lust because if it were love he'd never cheat on you." He now had my full attention.

"Excuse me."

"Yea earlier I was at Club Turquoise waiting for him and the other chick he fucks with was there and they looked very cozy."

"Yea right." He smirked.

"I knew I'd see you here and you wouldn't believe me, so I recorded it." He pulled his phone out.

"I swear these phone companies hit the lottery when they came out with this shit." He passed me the phone and sure enough there Remi stood with a woman in front of him. Her hands were under his shirt as he stared down at her. I pushed the phone back in his hand when she reached for Remi's jeans. I couldn't watch anymore.

"I told you." One single tear fell down my face and he took it as me being vulnerable. He reached out and hugged me. I struggled tryna get him off, pushed him back and ran up the steps.

"What's wrong? You ok?" Tara asked. She was at the top.

"I'm fine. Can I use your car to go?"

"Go? Why are you leaving?" She peeked around me and frowned her face up. She must've saw Ivan.

"Hey cuz!" Ivan moved past me and squeezed my ass. I smacked the shit outta him and he yoked me up.

"You obviously don't remember the last time." My feet were dangling as he continued choking me.

"Ivan get the fuck off her. What are you doing?" Tara was punching him in the back.

"YOOOO!" I saw Remi hit his brother and it knocked him out. Ivan's body hit the ground hard as hell. Luckily, the area we were in no one could see because I'm sure his guests would have a field day with this.

216

"You ok? What happened?" Remi was checking me over. I saw hands wrap around his waist.

"Baby, what's going on over here?"

"Baby?" I questioned and looked at the woman. I didn't have to say a word to know she's the one he was with earlier.

"Bitch you crazy?" Remi pushed her off.

"You weren't saying that earlier."

"What?" Remi turned around with the evilest look I've ever seen on him. It was worse than the one at the hospital.

"No need to deny it Remi. I saw the video. Tara can I have your keys please? I promise not to crash your car."

"You're not leaving Naima. She's lying." Remi tried pleading with me, but I saw the video.

"Is she? I mean that wasn't her who ran her hands under your shirt?" He didn't say a word.

"She wasn't tryna get your pants down at the restaurant earlier? Is that why you wanted to have sex before we came? Were you thinking about her?" Tara covered her mouth.

"You know what? It doesn't even matter. Why would I think a man who's never been in love could be faithful?

Goodbye Remi." I ran out the building and saw my mother pulling up. She never met Remi and I thought tonight would be perfect. I told her not to get out and I was leaving with her.

"What's going on here?" I heard before getting in the car. Some man stood there looking like an exact replica of Remi.

"Remington?" My mother spoke out the window in a confused tone.

"Remington who?" I questioned my mother because she couldn't be talking about the person I think she is.

"Nyeemah?" He asked the same thing and confused as well.

"Ma, please don't say this is who I think it is." My mother got out the car and walked over to him. Remi, his mom, Tara and another woman was standing there.

"Nyeemah?" Now his mother asked the same thing. Its like they couldn't believe their eyes.

"Its exactly who he is Naima. Here in the flesh. But how?" My mom didn't appear to be as upset as I thought she should be.

"No. No. No. No. It can't be." I walked over to where she was.

"Did you know Remi? Is that why you showed interest? You felt bad for me." I asked with tears falling down my face.

"Did I know what? What the fuck is going on?" Remi asked and no one said a word. His parents still seemed to be shocked at my mom showing up.

"How could you do me like that Remi? I loved you, I'm in love with you and this is how you repay me by keeping your father a secret."

"A secret? My father ain't no secret. You know all about him. I told you everything." I chuckled.

"Everything but the truth."

"The truth?"

"Yes, Remi the truth." He came closer to me.

"Naima, I admit the shit at the other club is suspect as fuck, but I can explain. As far as my father, there's nothing I didn't tell you about him."

"Oh, so you know he's the man who killed my father?"

219

Mario

"Her mom left so you're gonna have a few hours at the most." The guy said. Tonight, they had me going to retrieve whatever item it is from Naima's mother's house.

"Where's the stuff?" I asked referring to the sledgehammer and shit he said I needed to get behind the wall.

"Everything is on the side of her house in bushes."

"A'ight, I'm going now." I disconnected the call, ran down the steps and hopped in my car. I was finally healed after that nigga beat my ass at the gym. I ain't even mad because I was being petty.

I didn't know Naima moved on and hearing she did pissed me off. I also didn't expect the nigga to almost kill me either. I barely got one punch in. At least I know he'll protect her.

"WAIT!" Lina screamed out and ran to my car. She tried to get in and I kept the door locked.

"I'm coming too."

"Go back in the house Lina. Who the fuck gonna watch the kids?" She thought about what I said and backed away.

I pulled off thinking about how this is almost over. I can give Naima her house back, get rid of Lina and move on with my life. Its been nothing but a bunch of bullshit since Lina's been in my life and if I didn't know any better, I'd say she set all of it up. I know she ran her mouth about Naima, but she knows too much and been acting funny lately.

I drove past Ivy's house on the way and noticed mad cops, ambulances and coroners. I wonder what the fuck happened over there. I kept going until I reached Naima's mom house, parked down the street and prepared myself to be a damn demolition man. I still don't understand why these people couldn't do it. If they had that much power, they could've gone inside, tied her mom up and took it.

"Shit." I said to myself when I tripped over the curb. Hell yea I'm nervous. It may be dark out, but people are nosy.

I found the bag in the bushes and lifted the rug for the extra key. I only know its there because her mom stayed losing her keys. Naima told her to get one of those key boxes instead of putting it under the rug. I guess she didn't listen because here I am, entering the same spot my ex girl used to live in before getting her house.

I closed the door and made my way up the steps. It was a three-bedroom house and I had no idea which room he was talking about. I couldn't call back because the man always called from an unknown number. The only information they did give me is the spot is close to the closet. Each room only had one so it shouldn't be too bad. I took the sledgehammer out and started the process.

BOOM! BOOM! Each time I swung, the shit was loud as hell. I prayed no one heard me and called the cops.

The first room had nothing in it, neither did the second, which was the master bedroom. I went in the last one that held Naima's old room and smiled at the photos on her dresser. A few of them were of me and her.

When she moved out, she didn't take anything, and her mother must've left the room alone. I reminisced for a second about all the good times we used to have. My phone ringing brought me out my zone.

"Hello."

"Did you get it?" Lina asked.

Why you calling me?"

"Hurry up Mario. I don't want you to get caught."

"If you hang up, I can get back to it."

"Mario if she has new stuff bring it to me. I wore everything here already." I hung the phone up on her dumb ass. Hopefully, they take her out when I get whatever this is.

I swung the sledgehammer and the wall didn't break. In the other rooms it wasn't a problem, which led me to believe this is the spot. I broke the wall around it and ten minutes later a big black safe appeared.

"Well I'll be damned." I slid it out slowly and placed it on the bed. I pulled on the handle thinking it would be locked and it opened. My eyes grew wide when I looked inside.

"Police. Stay where you are." I heard from downstairs. Who the fuck called the cops on me? I started panicking and jumped out the window. I ran to my car through the back and sped outta there.

****

"Did you get it?" Lina asked with a grin on her face when I came in the door.

"YOU SET ME THE FUCK UP BITCH!" She took off running. I started to chase after her.

CLICK! I froze and almost shit on myself when I saw who it was. These motherfuckers are about to kill me.

To Be Continued....

CPSIA information can be obtained
at www.ICGtesting.com
Printed in the USA
LVHW092259260220
648289LV00003BA/371